Catbirds

Catbirds
Ezra Palmer

Published by Taag & Rohg Press
Los Angeles
www.taagandrohg.com

ISBN
979-8-9877882-0-2 Print
979-8-9877882-1-9 eBook
979-8-9877882-2-6 Audio

First Edition

to Jane

Catbirds

Stampede, maybe that would be the way to begin the eulogy, I thought, sitting in the first row of folding chairs at the front of the meeting room of the Amory Public Library, waiting for my mother and her husband to arrive for the memorial service, which was now two years too late, two years after my brother had died, two years after the fact, you might say, but Adam had died during the pandemic and we had put it off too long, and by now I wasn't sure if anyone would show up, our family had moved away from the town long ago, and besides, it had been two years since Adam died, not to mention the fact that Adam had been a difficult person, combative, litigious, tireless once he was engaged in a fight, for instance he kept folders of all his disputes, folders that I found in his dark little apartment after he died, the papers organized by dispute, many of them marked *FU* in the margins, which at first I thought stood for *Fuck You* but I learned, as I spent more time going through his things, that *FU* in fact stood for *Follow Up* but still, every time I saw *FU* written in his angry, jabbing hand, it was as if Adam was saying *fuck you* to me, yes, even now that he was dead, I could hear his voice in my head, saying *fuck you fuck you fuck you*, over and over, from the margins of his papers, but that would not be something to speak of at a memorial service, this was not the time to settle scores

Stampede, that was what Adam used to yell when he was a kid, *stampede*, he would call out, running down the hall toward me, and he meant it, probably, to be funny, at first, anyway, but he was so much bigger than me, he was a big child, a big boy, a big young man, the biggest of the brothers, the only one of us to play football, so he wasn't just heavy, he was heavy and muscular, plus he was two years older than me, and I have to admit he frightened me when he called out *stampede* as he ran down the hallway or the stairs, pounding down the stairs for breakfast, because he used to eat enormous amounts of food for breakfast, trying to put on weight for the football team, first the high school team, then the college team, every year he felt he needed to get bigger, but that turned into a problem after college, when he was no longer working out for hours at a time, instead he was sitting at a desk at an investment bank or a hedge fund, some kind of trading desk, I never really knew much about his work except that he made a great deal of money, although then he lost it, which was in contrast to his weight gain, that is, with money, he made a lot of it and then he lost it, unlike with the weight, which he put on and never took off, no, he just kept gaining weight, year after year, and although he was never really obese, like reality-television obese, he was overweight in an extremely unhealthy way, that is, it was just a matter of time before it killed him, I mean it would have killed him if not for the fact that

Stampede, *I remember Adam yelling that, running down the hall or pounding down the stairs of our old house in Amory, our childhood home,* it was meant to be funny, a joke, his catchphrase, the thing he yelled when he wanted to get somewhere before you, before any of the other boys could get there, *stampede,* it was a funny thing to yell, but it could be unnerving to hear him holler that way, because he was so big and so strong, and although he wasn't really fast, he was heavy and that gave him inertia, in other words he ran with a great deal of force, he was a football player after all, and I think he enjoyed the way his footsteps made so much noise, pounding down the hall, careening down the stairs, the stairway literally giving under his weight as he took the steps three or four at a time, the wood groaning, even cracking when he came down especially hard, and yet neither my mother nor my father told him to slow down, calm down, quiet down, they just let him run wild like that, at least as far as I can recall, for instance my father, if he was at home, remained in the sunroom or the attached porch, depending on the season, and my mother was either in the kitchen or smoking, smoking on the porch or in the little yellow room, a room behind the kitchen that we used to call the little yellow room, we called it the little yellow room because it had been painted a sunny yellow, although over the years it grew yellower and yellower, because that was where she stood and smoked

It was a wonder, I thought, sitting in the library meeting room, which we had reserved for a memorial service for Adam, that my mother had outlived any of her sons, given how much she had smoked, in fact the really amazing thing was that she hadn't burned the house down, because she left her cigarettes unattended, burning away unfinished in the ashtray, and as they burned they would tip back, falling on the counter or the floor or the tabletop, the house was scarred with cigarette burns, especially the little yellow room, that was where the downstairs phone was installed, the little yellow room behind the kitchen, where she stood smoking and talking on the phone, her smoky sanctuary, with the window looking out on the garage and the swing set in the backyard, the swing set where Adam challenged me to go higher, exactly in time with him, until the whole set pulled loose from the soil and tipped forward onto the grass, he knew what he was doing, even by himself he could make the swing set rock back and forth in the ground, that was his size but also his intensity, and also his age, by then he was ten or eleven, too big for the little swing set, anyway, he noticed that he could make the swing rock on its foundations, and he got it into his head that he could actually tip it over, and for days he swung and swung, jerking it this way and that, until he had the idea that the weight of two kids would pull it out of the ground, and it should have been Willie riding next to him in the second swing,

Willie was older than me, but Willie wouldn't do it, he would never do anything with Adam, so Adam told me to get in the other swing seat, and I did it, I always did what Adam told me to do, otherwise he would challenge me to a fight, and that's how I knocked out my tooth, not because he knocked it out with his fist, but because he turned out to be right about the swing, two boys swinging in unison was enough to yank it free from the ground, but this, too, was not something to speak of at a memorial service, the time Adam was responsible for my knocking my tooth out, although he contended that I had done it myself, I was the one who had fallen on my face when the swing set pulled loose and toppled in the backyard, I had known that the plan was to try to make it pull loose and topple, that was the way Adam's mind worked, he made legalistic arguments even as a boy, he had an argumentative nature and he loved to fight, probably because he was big and strong, not that he was a gifted athlete, no, he was a lineman on the high school football team, he never touched the ball, he only pushed forward, grunting and swearing, smashing against his opponents, pushing them back, what a perfect sport for him, it was how he approached his whole life, trying to knock over anything in his way, or even if it wasn't in his way, the point was to knock things over, and no wonder no one was coming to his memorial service, the room was still empty

Stampede, *that was Adam's catchphrase as a boy*, something he yelled around the house, and also at school, for instance I remember hearing him behind me in a school hallway, I was in sixth grade, the first day of my first year in middle school, and Adam was in eighth grade, the oldest grade in school, and when I heard his voice, unmistakably his voice, shouting *stampede* in the hallway behind me, I panicked and pushed against the wall to get out of his way, and in fact, I recalled as I sat in the folding chair at the library meeting room, I pissed myself, just a little, enough that there was a quarter-sized dark spot on my crotch, and I had to carry my backpack in an awkward way for the rest of the morning, until the spot dried and disappeared, the very first day of middle school, because when Adam yelled that, *stampede*, you had to get out of his way, the same way you had to cry *uncle* if he caught your little finger in his and somehow bent it back, in other words he was a bully, he bullied me and he bullied my younger brother, Evan, but he couldn't bully Willie that way, even though Willie also was younger than him, just by a year, Willie was wedged in between Adam and me, my mother had the three of us, *bang bang bang*, three of us in barely three years, first Adam then Willie then me, and Evan didn't come along for a good while after that, but Willie, even though he was younger than Adam and even though he was slim, no match, physically, for Adam, still, he was fierce and he wasn't afraid of fighting, he never seemed afraid of anyone but certainly not Adam, and he was willing to fight dirty, he would bite, he would scratch at other boys' eyes, he would claw or even kick at their balls, whatever it took to win a fight, so Adam tended to give Willie space, they mostly kept clear of one another, at home and at school, which was just as well, they had nothing in common, well, they had this library in common

Here we were, in the local library in Amory, the town where we grew up, another memorial service for another brother, more than twenty years later, almost thirty years ago it was when Willie died, he was just a sophomore in college, he died of AIDS, the drug treatments weren't available yet, if only he could have held on for a couple more years, who knows, he might still be alive, but the drugs weren't available yet, so he came home from college after a few semesters, and he was so thin, he had always been slight but he must have lost twenty-five pounds just in a few months, he had wanted to stay there at college, in North Carolina, he was studying costume design and he didn't want to come home, he wanted to stay in North Carolina, he wanted to die there, which was a bitter insult to my mother, or she took it that way, and as it was he could barely make the trip north, and he died hardly a month after he got home, he was skeletal at the end, and when he spoke you could see cloudy ropes of spit clinging to his lips and teeth, like his body was trying to keep his mouth closed, and then my parents rented the largest meeting room of the library, an auditorium, for a memorial service, and the room was packed, there must have been two hundred people, I remember people standing at the doors to the auditorium, unable to get into the room, craning their necks, it was tragic, a nineteen-year-old dying, dying of AIDS, and at that point my parents were still married, so all their friends were there, and Willie's high school friends, everyone from the theater department, it was a cliché for the gay boy to be involved with theater but he was, that was the truth of it, although he didn't want to act or sing, he designed costumes, he sewed costumes, not just for the high school productions but also for a community theater, in his senior year of high school the big production had been *Godspell*, and the entire cast attended his memorial service, they sang "Day by Day," there was not a dry eye in the auditorium, another cliché but it was true, everyone was crying, my father couldn't speak, he faltered at the podium, that was an early sign of his Huntington's, his voice slightly strangled, his balance iffy

Sitting in that same library, but almost thirty years later, I remembered that even Adam cried at Willie's memorial, which should not be surprising, of course anyone would cry at their brother's funeral, but Adam and Willie had never gotten along, and besides, Adam was a hard man, or he was practicing to be a hard man, as soon as he went away to college he had that aim of being a tough guy, a hard man, he had started wearing a wool overcoat, already dressing as if he worked on Wall Street, but actually, come to think of it, he had worked as an intern for a Wall Street firm that summer, I don't remember what firm it was, I was never really clear on what Adam did, even then it was mysterious, not only that but I had no curiosity about his internship, or his football team, or anything about him, I was mainly grateful that he was gone, out of the house, especially when Willie came home to die, which is what he did, that was the reason he was home, he was home to die, but Adam only visited once, because Willie didn't like him, had never liked him, and he never made a secret of the fact that he disliked Adam, even when he was dying he was cruelly honest about his dislike of Adam, saying why would I care if Adam came to visit, I'm sure Adam has better things to do than come back here to see me, and my mother said, don't talk like that, which was different from saying no, you're wrong, but it was obvious to her, it was obvious to anyone paying attention, that Willie despised Adam, which was interesting, because when we were children, I had despised Adam, I had been afraid of him so I despised him, but Willie, due to his fierceness, his willingness to bite and kick, was not so much afraid of Adam, in fact he had a way of seeming dismissive of Adam, as if he considered Adam almost insignificant, not really worthy of note, and of course Adam knew this and found Willie's haughtiness annoying or even enraging, but the point is that Willie actually hadn't seemed to despise Adam when we were boys in high school, it was only when he was dying that his feelings turned that way, with so little time left to him, with so little energy, with his body ravaged by AIDS, he seemed to decide that it would be best, it would be expedient, given his circumstances, to hate Adam, to go ahead and hate him, so for several weeks he did that, he deliberately despised Adam, and the one time that Adam came home from college to visit Willie, Willie used what little energy he had to tell him he shouldn't have bothered, that there was no reason for the two of them to sit together in the same room, so Adam stormed out and Willie, although he had barely any energy left at that point, managed to pick up his big paper McDonald's cup with a scowl of satisfaction and take a sip of his milkshake, which was the only thing he ate at the end, McDonald's milkshakes, we drove to the McDonald's in town and picked up vanilla milkshakes twice a day, although the cups mostly sat sweating, untouched, on his bedside table, but sometimes he managed to pick up the cup and take a sip, he was nineteen years old and he barely had the strength to lift a paper milkshake cup

When I recall Adam as a boy, I remember that he would yell stampede *when he was running down the upstairs hallway of the house,* up where our bedrooms were, boyland, my mother called it, the wild kingdom, she said, I never go up there if I can avoid it, she used to say, which was true, she seldom came upstairs, for instance when it came to laundry, she told us to bring our laundry downstairs, we dumped it all on the landing, yes, when our hampers were full we dumped our clothing on the landing, somehow that system was acceptable to my mother, she didn't mind that we left piles of clothing on the stairs, and she must have come upstairs occasionally but I don't recall her ever being in my room, my room that I shared with Evan, well, when I was sick, when I had a cold or the time I had Lyme disease, I remember her sitting on the edge of my bed, and later, with Willie, of course, she came to his room, although now that I recall it, she was not there very much, she had been hurt that he didn't want to come home to die, he had wanted to die at the infirmary at his college, where he was studying costume design, a dream come true, I imagined that college must have been a dream come true for Willie, it was a performing arts school, he had found a school that was basically one huge theater department, what better place for a boy like Willie, but he only was there for a short while, barely more than a full year, when he got sick, and then he struggled to stay there, he knew he was dying, everyone died of AIDS in those days, it was a death sentence, and he didn't want to come home, but in the end he had to, my mother and father drove down to North Carolina, to Willie's college, where he had grown skeletally thin, he was almost too weak to walk to the car, that was what my mother told me when she arrived home, she and I were in the little yellow room, where she smoked cigarettes, where she smoked cigarettes and spoke endlessly on the phone, she was as attached to that phone as she was to her cigarettes, but the night she got home with Willie, I stayed with her in the little yellow room while she paced and smoked and talked at me, they used to say that homosexuality was caused by the mother, she said to me, smoking and pacing in the little yellow room behind the kitchen, they don't believe that anymore, she said, they don't know what causes it, I don't know what causes it, I didn't understand him when he was a boy, I didn't realize it, it was different then, we didn't know anything about being gay then, I don't know why he's so angry at me, I didn't understand it, being gay, I should have known, now it's obvious, but it's too late now, he's angry at me, there's nothing I can do now, do you think he needs another milkshake, maybe we should make a trip to McDonald's before they close

And now here we are, I thought, back at the library, thirty years later, only this time for a memorial service for Adam instead of Willie, and instead of the auditorium, where hundreds of people could gather, we had reserved a smaller room, enough for maybe fifty people, because Willie had been so young, it seemed like the entire town had come to his memorial service, but with Adam it was a different story, he was almost fifty when he died, not an old man by any means, but it's different when a boy dies, Willie was just a boy, he wasn't even twenty yet, plus he died right there in Amory, tragic, everyone said, tragic, and by then Willie wasn't the only one getting AIDS, people knew a little about it by then, they weren't afraid of catching it off of him or me, well, that's not true, I imagine that some of them probably were at least a little afraid, in fact some of them may not have come to the memorial service, come to think of it, but still there were more than two hundred people at Willie's service, but with Adam I doubted that more than a handful of people would show up, and I turned in my metal folding chair to look back at the room, and no, there was no one there yet, although it was early still, early enough that even my mother hadn't arrived, although she would not arrive early for Adam's service, I didn't think, she and Adam had had a difficult relationship, yes, Adam was a difficult person and he and my mother had had a difficult relationship, he hated her smoking

in the house, he insisted she smoke on the porch, or if she had
to smoke inside, it had to be in the little yellow room, and
that was why she only smoked in there, that was why she spent
all of her time in there, talking on the phone and smoking,
because Adam had insisted that she not smoke anywhere else,
he was only seven or eight when he began complaining about
her smoke, but the rest of us, as I recalled it, didn't mind so
much, well, I didn't love it but it didn't drive me crazy, but
for Adam the smell was toxic, he used that word, *toxic*, he was
only seven or eight and somehow he was familiar with the word
toxic, did you learn that word in school, my mother asked him,
but he refused to talk with her if she was smoking, and in the
end he really did push her back into the little yellow room, that
was Adam for you, he was argumentative from the first, one
of my earliest memories is the day Willie hit Adam over the
ear with a block and Adam responded by hitting him, *whipping*
him, essentially, with a length of Hot Wheels track, he whipped
him with a yard-long plastic track, it made a whistling sound
in the air and struck Willie across the side of the face, and
Willie grabbed at his cheek and fell over in a crouch, but he
didn't cry, I don't remember Willie ever crying as a boy, come
to think of it, and after a moment he sprang at Adam, and
they pulled at each other's hair and punched each other, they
were only five or six at the time, I suppose, and I was four, and
I thought they might kill each other, I actually thought that
one or the other of them, belligerent Adam or fierce Willie,
would somehow kill the other, strangle his brother to death or
beat his head on the ground until his skull cracked, and if I am
remembering it correctly, the really eerie thing about the way
my brothers fought was that they did it silently, for instance
Willie didn't make a sound when the Hot Wheels track struck

his cheek, even though it left a visible mark he didn't cry out, he only bent over to recover in silence, and when the two of them entangled and fell on the floor, punching and clawing, they still didn't say anything, as I remember it, in fact I think that my memory must be accurate, because the next thing I recall was my mother responding to the sound of my crying, why is Randy crying, she called out, she was probably all the way on the other side of the house, in the little yellow room, smoking and talking on the telephone, but she came jogging down the hallway, calling, Randy, are you all right, and Willie and Adam disentangled themselves from each other by the time she appeared in the doorway, and my mother could see they must have been fighting, their hair was mussed and their cheeks were mottled, in fact Willie's face had a bright-red stripe, two inches wide, where he had been hit by the Hot Wheels track, but I was the only one who made any noise, and if I remember accurately both Willie and Adam were angry at me, I had disturbed their fight, I had interrupted it for them, I really think that each of them wanted to have it out once and for all, they were only five or six years old then but there was the sense that one of them would have to go, one would have to kill the other, or at least prove final domination, and my crying had brought my mother into the room before they could settle the matter, so the question of dominance, of primacy, of *survival*, would have to wait for another day, anyway, when Willie died at the age of nineteen, a part of me thought it was a miracle he had survived that long, but the surprising thing about their feud was that it ended because Willie showed a level of viciousness that even Adam had not anticipated, not even Adam, who was so cruel to Willie, and so angry at him, consumed with rage, even so he probably would not have taken

it to the level that Willie did, when they were ten years old,
I think it was, and after that they had an unspoken truce, or
I suppose that in fact Willie had won, all he wanted was for
Adam to leave him alone, and he achieved that goal

I'm Randy Green, that's how to start it, I thought, sitting in the folding chair in the library meeting room, *thank you for coming today, for those of you who don't know me, I'm Randy Green, I'm Adam's younger brother*, well, that would assume that anyone other than family comes to this service, two years after the fact, two years since Adam died, they found him floating in that filthy canal in Ogden, face down he was floating, not that the police provided any details about that, I had to do my own investigation, if that's the word, I looked into it, I asked around, I found the man who had found Adam, that was how I knew that Adam had been found floating face down in the water, and I knew exactly where Adam was found, floating in that canal in Ogden, the water a murky greenish brown, rainbow slicks across the surface of the water, I imagined him lying there, face down, in an iridescent slick of engine oil, the seagulls chattering on the pilings above the canal, face down in that water, lying there dead just a few miles from the site of his greatest triumph, Yale University, he had set himself the goal of going to Yale, and somehow he had managed it, he was not necessarily a brilliant student but he was dogged, anger and resentment drove that, he was smart enough and hardworking, and of course he was large-bodied and strong, a decent football player, offensive and defensive line, he played both ways in high school, I suppose that made a difference as well, in any case getting into Yale, attending Yale, that was the apex for him, his grand achievement, but thirty years later he was floating face down in the dirty water of a canal off the Housatonic River

Face down in the dirty water of a canal, I thought, as I sat by myself at the front of the meeting room at the Amory Public Library, hunched over in the chair, and I thought that as Adam's brother I should at least turn my shoulders toward the doorway, or, I thought, I should stand by the door to greet people, someone would have to stand and greet people at the door, and it would probably have to be me, here I was, the first of the family to arrive, no one else was here, including my mother and her husband, Carl, Cary and Carl, the third time is the charm, my mother said of Carl, of her marriage to Carl, they lived in Vermont, in what had been Carl's family's vacation house, somehow my mother was still alive despite all the cigarettes she smoked, all the time she spent smoking in the little yellow room of our house in Amory, she outlived two of her sons, I thought, glancing behind me at the meeting room, still empty, the rows of folding chairs facing the lectern, and I remembered that I would need to go behind that lectern to unroll the pull-down screen for a slide show, I wondered if I should turn on the slideshow before the guests arrived, if they should be called guests, mourners is the word, I thought, normally mourners would be the word to use for guests at a memorial service, but it seemed unlikely that anyone would actually be mourning Adam today, well, no, there would be one person, I corrected myself, there would be one person, but that was a paltry count for someone who had lived nearly fifty years, one person to mourn your loss for fifty years of life, but that was Adam, he had burned through virtually every bit of goodwill the world had offered him, burned through his family, his marriage, his business partners, in the end he was even feuding with the owners of his apartment complex, the Treadway, the building was called, it had a name, for some reason, as if it were a grand property, but it wasn't grand, it was a six-floor apartment building, mostly retirees, it seemed, dim halls and a shuddering elevator, that was where Adam finished off his life, having risen so high so fast, he ended up in a cramped apartment in Ogden, and he died in Ogden, drowned there, literally

The cops were no help, they had no curiosity, there was a pandemic, the local hospital was backed up, then the pathologist came down with it, Covid-19, and there were demonstrations, Black Lives Matter, Adam died amid all that, well, he had died a few weeks earlier but it had taken a while to identify him, anyway, no one seemed to be interested in looking into the circumstances of his death, the police had other fish to fry, so to speak, I was the only one asking any questions, the cops didn't seem to see any reason to ask questions, and to be fair, they were busy, they were overwhelmed, I couldn't even get into the station for the first two days, and even then I could see they didn't want me there, they were impatient with me, dismissive, they dismissed my questions, when I asked about the cuts and scrapes on Adam's face, the postmortem on Adam had mentioned cuts on his face, why did he have cuts and bruises on his face, I wanted to know, had he been in a fight, I asked, and the cop, the detective, Detective Manfredi was his name, Detective Manfredi said to me, why, was your brother the type to get in fights, did he get in a lot of fights, to your knowledge, well, Adam did get in fights, he spent his life fighting, but not fistfights, I told the cop, Detective Manfredi, but he wasn't listening, there were noises out on the street, and meanwhile his mask was pulled down under his nose, which at the time was alarming, I didn't want to sit there in the precinct house, cops wandering around in riot gear, no one had a mask on properly, a lot of them weren't wearing masks at all, and there were firecrackers going off somewhere nearby, I assumed they were firecrackers, and I could hear protesters chanting as well, and the cop, the detective, I mean, looked at me over his half-worn paper mask, he had bloodshot eyes, he seemed tired, he wasn't a bad guy, not really, but he wasn't concerned about the circumstances of Adam's death, I just want to understand the cuts on his face, I said, and he said something about bobbing in the water, Adam's face must have banged up against the pilings, the tide had pushed him against the rough wood, he said, that's what we figure, or it might just have been the way he fell, he might have banged his face as he fell, and I said, so you don't think he was pushed, and the detective said, why, he said, did your brother have a lot of enemies

Enemies, well, the first name that came to mind was my mother, not that I told the detective that, but when he asked about enemies my first thought was, well, my mother, she never got along with Adam, or to be honest she was mean to him, she insulted him, she insulted him to his face, she had no patience for him, for instance, when he was a baby, she had said, he cried all the time, he was colicky, I just never knew what to do with him, that's what she used to say about Adam, I just never knew what to do with him, and then there was the disaster, that was the word my mother used, the disaster, of her getting pregnant just six months after Adam was born, that was Willie, who arrived before my mother was ready for him, he was delicate and anxious as a baby, that was how my mother recalled it, he needed her attention, and Adam, she used to recall, did not, he did not need her attention, not the same way, she said, Adam was always involved in his projects, she recalled, and I asked her once, Mom, I said, how could he have been involved in projects if he was only a year or two old, well, I don't know, she said, that's just the way he was, he always had something he was doing, he was so independent, I remember when I first took him to nursery school, he simply walked away from me, he didn't look back, she said, not even once, the other children were clinging to their mothers, some were crying, but Adam just walked away without even saying goodbye, I don't think he approved of me, she said, he didn't approve of my smoking, he used to read from the warnings on the cigarette package, he was very judgmental about that, she said, he was puritanical about my smoking and drinking, and when he got older he claimed that he was allergic to cigarette smoke, my god, she said, he was always at it, he was always making his opinions known, I don't know why, we were just very different sorts of people, and I mean, think of it, he voted for Trump, he told me he would vote for Trump again, if you can believe that, she said, but regardless of politics we didn't see eye to eye on almost anything, she told me, and when my mother told me that, when she recalled that Adam had told her that he planned to vote for Trump and not Biden, I was surprised that they had spoken as recently as that, they never spoke any longer, they hadn't spoken for years, to my knowledge, as, similarly, my younger brother, Evan, had not spoken with Adam in years, no one spoke with Adam except me, not that I spoke with him very often but I tried, I tried to stay in touch, I felt vaguely guilty that Evan and my mother and I remained in contact with one another, even if we didn't see each other very often, we were in contact, but neither of them were in contact with Adam, and he was divorced and childless and it made me sad to think of him being alone like that, although if I'm being one hundred percent honest, pretty much every time I saw him I walked away in a rage, or at least in a bad mood, almost every time, and I wondered why I bothered, but neither Evan nor my mother ever contacted him, or at least they hadn't to my knowledge, so I asked her about the Trump conversation, when was that, I asked her, was that during the pandemic, and she said yes, or no, wait, I can't remember, and I said, did you call him or did he call you, and she looked at me, she had an extravagantly wrinkled face, wrinkled I imagine not just from the years she had lived but the smoking and of course the divorce and the deaths in the family, she hadn't had an easy life, anyway, she stared at me and pursed her lips and made a little shaking motion with her head, as if a mosquito were buzzing in her ear, and she didn't answer me, so I didn't find out whether she had called him or he had called her, to her it didn't matter

It didn't matter if my mother had called Adam or if Adam had called her, I thought, glancing back at the meeting room of the Amory Public Library once again to see if anyone had arrived, but they hadn't, I was still the only one there, I had thought it would be a good thing for someone to arrive early, someone in the family should arrive early, I thought, someone should be there to greet guests, there was no knowing what time people might arrive, and I knew that my mother would not want to be bothered, just to drive down from Vermont for his memorial service was a lot to ask of her, that was as much as she would be willing to do on Adam's behalf, because she and Adam were never friendly, I don't think ever, and in fact they were enemies, enemies was a word that came to mind because of what the detective had asked me, did your brother have a lot of enemies, but I could see that he was just passing the time with me, he didn't think Adam had enemies, not the kind of enemies who would hit him over the head and leave him for dead in a canal off the Housatonic River, that was not something my mother would do, or could even physically manage, with her lungs and her bad back, she walked at an odd angle now, like a wading bird in a marsh, and she had to stop for breath every now and then, her breathing was quite ragged, especially when she walked, but even when she was just standing, say at a kitchen counter, you could hear the air working its way through her windpipe, it was a kind of anguished, tidal sound, anyway, if

Adam had been attacked, if he had been assaulted, hit over the head and knocked into the river to drown, it wasn't my mother who did it, even though they were enemies, in their way, sad to say, a mother and son, enemies, but they had been enemies almost all their lives, just as Adam and Willie had always been enemies, as far as I know, they had never just been friendly brothers, they had always squabbled, and if Willie had not been so cold, cold and vicious, I wonder what Adam might have done to him, really that was something to think about, if Willie hadn't done what he did, with the pencils, and frightened Adam so badly that he simply left Willie alone after that, if Willie hadn't been so coldly vicious, who knows, Adam might have beaten him up in a rage, he might have actually killed him, Willie had a way of enraging Adam to the point that Adam quivered, like a bowstring drawn taut, and he would charge at Willie, who was so graceful and quick, Adam did not always catch him, but if he did, Willie would immediately poke at Adam's eyes, or worse, they fought in silence, that way our parents would not hear it, it was like they had a pact to fight in silence, the only sound they made was if they accidentally knocked something over, they were only eight or nine, wrestling and punching in almost complete silence, just little grunts and puffs of breath, I was younger but not by much, and all I could do was shy away from the two of them, keep my distance, I was frightened of Adam but to be honest I was slightly frightened by Willie too, something about his implacable coldness, he didn't treat me badly, but he mainly ignored me, the way he ignored Adam, which enraged Adam, but I was grateful to be ignored, I didn't understand Willie, I didn't understand why he acted, as I thought of it, like a girl, but I knew that when people teased him he would fight them, he was suspended from school several times, but I didn't understand why he wore the clothes he wore, of course he would be teased, why did he wear what he wore, for instance a chiffon scarf of my mother's, why would he wear that to school, he must have known the other children would tease him, they teased *me*, as if I were the one wearing the scarf, anyway, if anyone made a remark Willie would start fighting, he had hard little fists and somehow he always seemed to win his fights, I guess it was because he fought dirty, it wasn't just with Adam that he fought dirty, so he always won his fights, he would push boys' faces into the dirt, he did it to girls, too, actually, he must have beaten up eight or nine children over the years, and by the time he started middle school nobody challenged him, and I think he got through middle school and high school relatively easily, but as for Adam, he and Willie were enemies, certainly, even if they had an unspoken truce, but Willie had been dead just over twenty-five years by the time Adam died, so Willie couldn't have been the one to knock him unconscious and leave him floating in the dirty canal, Willie couldn't have done it and my mother couldn't have done it, obviously, not that I ever thought she had, it was just a thought I had, remembering the detective at the Ogden police asking if Adam had enemies

I didn't know if Adam had other enemies, although it seemed plausible, but I knew that he did have a gun, I had found a gun in his apartment when I was cleaning it out after he died, a handgun in his bureau drawer, there was a handgun in there with his polo shirts, he had accumulated a huge number of polo shirts, which I boxed up and donated to the Goodwill, they were all XL and XXL, too big for me, too big for Evan, and there was something creepy about even thinking about wearing his clothes, and I remembered, then, sitting in the front row of the meeting room of the library, that I was supposed to be composing a brief eulogy for Adam, there was no one else to do it, *stampede*, I thought, maybe I should abandon that idea as an opening, I should probably just be factual, there was no point in trying to be engaging or funny, that kind of speech would not suit Adam, not under the circumstances, *Adam was born*, I could say, *in 1973*, yes, I should recite the particulars of his life and that would be enough, *he was born in New Haven County in 1973, the oldest of four sons of Rafe and Cary Green, and as a boy he was a passionate football player and a fan, a fan of the New York Giants, which was an unpopular choice in our town, where everyone rooted for the New England Patriots*, well but enough about football, or no, *he loved being a part of the football team in high school, that was his greatest pride, becoming the captain his senior year, an honor that reflected his passion for the team and for the sport*, not that he was a particularly gifted athlete, no, he just tried harder than anyone, worked harder than anyone, as a freshman he set a goal for himself that he would become a captain of the football team, even though he knew he wouldn't play any of the glamorous positions, the skill positions, as they call them, he would never be the quarterback or a receiver or a linebacker, no, he just lined up on the offensive line and the defensive line and pushed and shoved, game after game, playing both ways, and he was a captain his senior year, and when he went to Yale after graduating he was nothing more than a walk-on, but he was on the team all four years, it was admirable, *Adam actually set two goals for himself when he started his freshman year in high school, the first was to become a captain of the football team, and the second was to win admission to Yale University, and he achieved both of those ambitions, which is a testament to his focus, his drive, his hard work* and his humorlessness, his single-minded zeal, that was why he yelled *stampede*, he needed everyone to get out of his way, although it really was meant to be humorous, *stampede*

I remembered, sitting at the front of the meeting room at the Amory Public Library, the last time I had heard Adam call *stampede*, it had been eight years ago, when he was living in Norwalk, in a condo in Norwalk, a pretty nice place with a community pool and tennis court, it was nice, albeit a step down from the house he had owned when he was married, but the marriage was over and the house had been sold and now he was a single man, a divorced man, living in a condo complex in Norwalk, it wasn't a fancy town compared to some other New York suburbs, and he was ashamed of living there, in a condo, I think he was ashamed, although it was a perfectly nice place, a two-bedroom town house, a nice pool, in fact I spent the afternoon with Adam at the pool, and it was almost like a private pool, there was just us at one end and two children with their mother at the other end, we basically had the place to ourselves and it was a nice spot to spend a summer afternoon, but Adam was sour about the condo, the construction quality was shoddy, he said, he was feuding with the management company, he said, of course he was feuding with the management company, I thought, but I set that thought aside, I was in the pool, the water was cool, it was highly chlorinated, my eyes stung, but it was a relief to be out of the heat, and I suggested that Adam jump in but he wouldn't, he wanted to talk about my finances because I was going through a hard patch, as they say, I was separated from my wife, Daphne and I had separated, Daphne had had an affair and I moved out, and Adam insisted on giving me financial advice, he was fixated on it, he said he knew how to handle the situation because he was divorced, he had been through a divorce, and he wanted me to learn from his experience, and it was dreadful for me to hear him say that, because it was already awful to be separated from Daphne, and even worse to think that in this way I was like my brother, he was divorced and now I might be, too, how awful, I thought, because I could understand why Adam would have gotten divorced, of course he would never have a lasting marriage, I thought, but I was different, I thought, I had been in a loving and stable relationship, I had a child, my daughter, Muriel, Em we called her, I was not the kind of person to get divorced, I thought, although Adam was, he was the sort of person to get divorced, I thought, anyway, Daphne and I were separated at the time and Adam wanted to give me advice, he wanted to set up some kind of offshore account, if I understood him properly, and I was trying to be polite and listen to him, why, I didn't know, I was the only person in the family in contact with Adam, I made a point of contacting him when I was back on the East Coast, I lived in California but I made a point of arranging to see him when I was in New York, it wasn't much trouble to take Metro-North to Greenwich or Norwalk or wherever he was living, and now I was separated from my wife, and Adam had advice for me, he told me that Daphne would try to destroy me, she would try to take everything I had, not that I had anything, and besides, it wasn't true, we were separated but we weren't at war, but apparently that was what had happened to Adam, his wife had tried to take everything he had, or at least that was Adam's opinion about what had happened when his marriage failed, Celeste, her name was, according to Adam Celeste had tried to destroy him and take everything he had, so he assumed that Daphne would do the same to me, and I didn't have the energy to try to persuade him that I was not him, Daphne was nothing like his wife, the two of us, Daphne and I, were talking about getting therapy, we were separated but we were discussing therapy, but Adam was adamant that I needed to stash some money, maybe all my money, not that I had much money, in an account somewhere that, he said, would not be traceable in the U.S., that was the phrase he used, the funds would not be traceable in the U.S., which sounded illegal to me, but I didn't say so, because Adam would be upset if I said that to him, and as he talked and talked about this untraceable fund, whatever it was, I just let myself slip under the water of the pool, I felt the cool chlorine tingling around my eyelids, it was dispiriting to be separated from my wife, I didn't want to be separated from her, and it was also dispiriting to hear Adam hectoring me to move my money into some semilegal scheme that he was privy to, so I ducked down, out of the way of his words, which I shouldn't have done, I was as good as saying I wasn't listening to him, and when I surfaced, of course he was angry, he was scowling, he said, can we stop with the dipshit act, and I wondered why I had bothered, why had I gone to the trouble of taking the train to Connecticut when all I got out of it was Adam calling me a dipshit, a dipshit who was about to be fleeced by my soon-to-be ex-wife, and I held up my hands, like I give up, you win, and I said, Adam, forget about my marriage, forget about Daphne, forget about my finances, it's a sunny day, it's hot, the water's fine, come jump in the pool, and he said something about it being a crap pool, because his old house, the house he had owned before, with his ex-wife, Celeste, had a pool, a spectacular pool, I remember it had been wired for sound, with speakers in the box bushes ringing the pool and speakers actually embedded in the walls of the pool, somehow they transmitted music in the water, although apparently a neighbor was bothered by the noise, of course a neighbor would be bothered by the noise, of course Adam would get in a fight with his neighbor, but the point is it was a really fancy pool, not like this plain one that I was bobbing in, a simple rectangular pool with a concrete apron and a few mesh chairs and chaises arranged around the edge, it wasn't fancy enough for Adam, it wasn't exclusive enough, he had experienced a different level of luxury, I supposed, but I said, Adam, it's not a crap pool, the water is perfect, come on, take a swim, relax, and he stood up, oh, he had gained so much weight by then, he was big, his swimsuit was digging into his belly, but he stood up and put a foot in the water, it's nice, he said, and before I knew it he yelled *stampede* and he leapt, he leapt right over me, he cannonballed into the pool, it was a prodigious splash, and when he surfaced he squirted a little water at me, he had a trick he could do with cupped hands, he squirted me and I swept some water at him and we just splish-splashed like that, I don't know for how long, but we did, in his condo pool in Norwalk, splish-splashing, for once we were just acting like brothers

He could swim, so why did he drown, I wondered, glancing back again at the library meeting room, still empty, and at this point it seemed possible no one would come to pay their respects, just the family, what was left of it, *that* made a certain amount of sense, hardly anyone would mourn Adam, it made sense that no one would bother to come to a memorial service for him, especially now that it was two years since he had died, why even bother at this point, why even, to be honest, *pretend* to mourn him, he had been so bellicose, yes, warlike, that described Adam, his whole life was a series of battles that added up to a single war, I supposed he had lost the war in the end, floating face down in a canal off the Housatonic River, that was the end of Adam's long war and he had lost, although by that measure I guess we all lose in the end, even if we don't end up face down in a filthy, oil-slicked backwater, but why had he drowned, if he could swim, I wanted to ask the police about this but the detective, Detective Manfredi, didn't find it mysterious, your brother fell, he said, he banged his head, he scraped his face on the pilings, most likely, but why didn't he have his wallet, I wanted to know, Detective Manfredi didn't have the answer, and he didn't care, it wasn't a big town but for some reason the police had tear-gassed a protest march, there was a faint scent of tear gas in the air at the police station, Detective Manfredi's eyes were red-rimmed, he had been hit with some gas, I guessed, my own eyes felt vaguely itchy, there was too much going on, Black Lives Matter, lockdowns, Covid-19, and amid all that Adam was found floating in a canal off the Housatonic River, it wasn't really surprising that no one was paying much attention to Adam's death, not amid all that, and it wasn't as if Adam was some rich guy at that point, he was pretty much broke, he was behind on his rent, he was feuding with the management company, he hadn't worked in more than two years, I could imagine that the police would just shrug off his death, some broke and lonely fifty-year-old man who lived in a dingy apartment building, he went to Yale, I told Detective Manfredi, I don't know if you knew this but my brother attended Yale, I don't know why I said it, it was just that Detective Manfredi didn't seem to be paying any attention, maybe if Adam seemed like a big deal, maybe that would make his death more urgent, and two years later I cringed to remember that I had told Detective Manfredi that Adam had attended Yale, I said it to this cop who was a stranger to me, a stranger to my brother and my family, I don't know what was going through my mind to tell him that Adam had gone to Yale, but Detective Manfredi didn't even seem to hear what I had said, he had other things on his mind, your brother's wallet probably fell out of his pocket when he was in the water, Detective Manfredi said, and I never got any more information from the cops, I had Detective Manfredi's card, but I didn't call him, I didn't call him the next day when I was clearing out Adam's bedroom drawers and found a pistol under his polo shirts, and when I came across the gun I wondered if I should call Detective Manfredi, but I remembered his red-rimmed eyes and the firecrackers going off somewhere near the police station, and I knew the police wouldn't care that Adam had a gun, they wouldn't find it strange, but it surprised me to find a gun in Adam's apartment, it didn't fit in with my image of

Adam, yes, he was warlike, but it was bullying and legalisms, threats and shouting, lawsuits, he had been involved in half a dozen lawsuits, maybe more, but that was different from needing a gun, I didn't know why he would have a gun, and that was when I began investigating, if that's the word, investigating the circumstances of his death, no one else was going to do it amid a pandemic and nationwide marches, George Floyd, Black Lives Matter, what was Adam compared to the chaos of the moment, Adam floating face down in the water, he wasn't a priority for anyone, and even for me he wasn't a priority, he hadn't been a priority, but he was my brother, the condition of his head, his face all banged up, no wallet in his pocket, drowned in a canal off the Housatonic River, and why did he have a gun in his bedroom drawer, I had so many questions about Adam's death, it was unnerving for him to die that way, never mind that he and I hadn't gotten along and rarely saw each other, we were brothers, although my other brother, my younger brother, Evan, didn't see it that way, he took, you could say, Detective Manfredi's attitude, who cares, he said, when I showed him the gun I found in Adam's bureau, who cares if Adam had a gun, what difference is it to you, what difference is it now, he said, now that he's dead, and he was right, Evan was right, it didn't make any difference, but still I couldn't stop wondering about it, about the gun and the scrapes on his face and the missing wallet, where was the wallet, maybe in the canal, and also, amid the polo shirts, in the same drawer with the gun, there was a note, a gift card, to Adam, from someone named Julia, and I wondered who Julia was, she had signed her note, love, Julia, and after the police told me they weren't interested, if not in so many words, I found the gun and the note from someone named Julia, and I found myself looking into why Adam had died, even though I didn't care, really, but I wondered

My little brother didn't care at all, there were just the two of us now, but he didn't care, he wanted to clear out Adam's apartment and try to settle with the landlord as quickly as possible, let's just get this over with, Evan said, he wanted to get back to his own life in Philadelphia, he had never gotten along with Adam, well, he was no different from anyone else in the family, and he hadn't spoken with Adam in more than ten years, not that they had ever been close, for one thing they were almost seven years apart, Evan never really interacted much with Adam, but he was frightened of him, frightened of Adam's moods, Adam's bad temper, and he wasn't tough, Evan wasn't tough, the way Willie had been tough, Willie had decided early on that the only way to deal with Adam was head-on, to meet him with violence if necessary, and one afternoon when Adam had shoved him, I don't know why but Adam and Willie always tried to sit at the same worktable in the living room, so Adam shoved him, and what Willie did was he stabbed Adam, he stabbed him with a pencil, it doesn't sound like much but he drove it deep into Adam's thigh, I don't know how deep but it was deep, Willie could be savage, and he drove a sharpened pencil into Adam's thigh, and then, when Adam reached up for Willie's face, even as he gripped his thigh in agony, Willie was ready, he had prepared *two* pencils, and he drove his second pencil into Adam's palm, he was calm when he did it, Adam was doubled over, he was bleeding from his thigh and from his hand, he was sobbing, and Willie said to him, I told you to leave me alone when I'm working at this table, he said it so calmly, in retrospect his calmness, his quiet voice, was disturbing, he was only ten years old, if I remember right, in retrospect I wonder if Willie had mental problems of his own, maybe both he and Adam had some kind of anger problem, some kind of pathology, although Willie was dealing with a hostile world, it wasn't easy being gay back then in Amory, Connecticut, even in our family, he knew it long before the rest of us, still, to coldly stab Adam that way, not once but twice, clearly he had been sitting at the table waiting for Adam to disturb him, he had one sharpened pencil in either hand, and he didn't just poke Adam, he stabbed him, it was lucky for Adam that Willie hadn't aimed for his face, but anyway, the two pencils did it, Adam mostly left Willie alone after that, they essentially ignored each other, although of course Adam continued to bully me, not as often or as fiercely as he had bullied Willie, Willie was probably right to respond the way he did, disturbing as it was, that was how you had to manage Adam when he was a boy, Willie had the ferocity to stand up to Adam, but I didn't, and Evan certainly didn't, especially because he was so much younger, all he could really do was cower in Adam's presence, and for the most part Adam was satisfied with that, I thought, so no wonder when Adam died Evan didn't even pretend to be sorry, he only came along to Adam's apartment with me as a favor, as far as he was concerned we could burn Adam's belongings, and he wasn't interested in finding out how Adam had died, he didn't wonder why Adam had drowned even though he knew how to swim, or why Adam had a gun in his bedroom, or who this Julia woman was, who had given Adam a gift and signed it, love, Julia, Evan didn't care about any of that, he just wanted to clear the apartment out and go home, who knows why Adam had a gun, he asked me, who cares, he said, while we stuffed Adam's clothes in plastic bags to be dropped off at the Goodwill, I was checking the pockets, I had found the gun, I had found the note from someone named Julia, I couldn't help it, I wanted to know, but Evan didn't even care about looking in the pockets of Adam's clothes before bagging them up, what do you think you'll find in there, he said, do you think you'll find clues, he made it sound silly that I should be looking for information about Adam's death, and I could understand it, he hated Adam, he had always hated Adam, he didn't try to stay in touch with Adam the way I did, he could never believe that I made a point of visiting Adam once every year or two, why would you waste your time like that, he said, why waste another minute on Adam, and I remembered, sitting in the public library in Amory, I remembered when Adam went to college, Evan started calling him *Klondike*, what did it mean, I never knew where the name came from, but for some reason it bothered Adam, when he heard Evan call him *Klondike*, he smiled, but I could see it bothered him, *Klondike*, Evan would mutter at him, *Klondike*, and Adam smiled, he grimaced a little like he was smiling, now that he was in college it wasn't like he was going to punch or shove Evan, he was too old for that now, really what Adam was focused on was, at that point, his life at college, and even more than that, on getting a job on Wall Street, he already had some kind of summer job on Wall Street, whatever it was he did on Wall Street, Adam was focused on getting out, getting out of the family, and I guess the family was, by and large, happy to have him go, even my mother and father, even they were basically happy to have him out of the house, there was just a lack of connection, and Evan detested Adam, and Willie was dead, and my father was getting sick by then, and a few years later my mother just left, even though

Dad could barely take care of himself by then, he moved to an apartment building in New Haven, he needed a place where there were no stairs, and in the end it was Evan who lived with Dad, after college he moved in with Dad, and the two of them lived together, Evan painting and drawing in what had been the dining area, and my father spending most of his time on a balcony off the living room, in warm weather anyway, they lived together for two years, until Dad died, and at that point I was in California, and Adam was somewhere in New York City, once Dad was gone Evan moved to Philadelphia, it was like someone had set a bomb under our house and we just exploded, like shrapnel, that was that, it was as if there never had been a family, we just scattered, and sometimes I wondered if I was the only one who cared, I was the one who initiated calls, I made a point of visiting Evan and Mom and even Adam, well, Evan and Mom still talked regularly, he was her baby, her fourth child, her fourth and last child, they spoke on the phone almost every day, I spoke with her, what, once every two or three weeks, she almost never called me, I had to call her, with Evan it was different, he was her baby, they spoke all the time, but no one spoke with Adam, no one called him, I was the only one, I visited him every year or two, I made a point of calling him every once in a while, not that I wanted to speak with him, exactly, but a part of me felt like I had to do it, I had to maintain the bond with him, he was my brother after all, we sometimes had a nice time together, splish-splashing in his pool after I separated from Daphne, that had been, what, five, maybe six years before he died

I felt sorry for Adam, as I grew older I felt sorry for him, as big a pain in the ass as he was, I pitied him, he was all alone, he had alienated everyone in his life, and once I was an adult I was able to look back at our childhood and feel some sympathy for him, for the way Mom had treated him, she never liked him and he, in turn, never liked her back, although there was no excusing his behavior, not really, but I tried to stay in touch with him, I was the only one left in the family who tried to stay in touch with him, for instance I called him at the beginning of the lockdown, as it was called at the time, the lockdown, I knew he was alone in an apartment in Connecticut, I hadn't been there, I hadn't visited him at his last address, I knew he saw it as another step down for him, a big step down, once he had owned a huge house in Greenwich, a mansion, basically, and even after his divorce he had a nice enough condo, but his bad luck kept running, no, that's not it, he just kept picking fights with the wrong people, not fistfights, but legal battles, and he had no way to make money, as he saw it he had no way to make money because he had been barred from the securities industry, I remember him using that phrase, barred from the securities industry, but he thought he could find a way around the ruling, I didn't know what he was up to, exactly, except that he was caught and fined again, money he didn't have, and for a long time he had his own firm, as he called it, he referred to it as a firm but as far as I know neither he nor the firm did anything, he wanted to be a financial adviser, but he was barred from the securities industry so I don't imagine anyone would hire him, I don't know that it would be legal for him to charge for his services, he tried to get me to hire him, or invest, I didn't know, I didn't have any money as it was, I had changed careers, I was just getting started in my new career as a therapist, I had been a writer, I had been a screenwriter, not a very successful writer but not a failure, and then I went back to school to become a therapist, and I was still building up my practice, but Adam was convinced that I had a great deal of money, it was understandable because I had written a story that was made into a movie, a long time ago I wrote a story, "Catbirds," about Willie, well, it had been about the whole family, my mother and my father and Adam and Willie and me and Evan, the four of us in a row, Willie and Adam at each other's throats, and then Willie's death and the entire implosion, or explosion, I don't know, of the family, my mother leaving my father, she moved out when he got sick, in any case, I wrote the story, and my former screenwriting partner thought it would make a good script, in fact he was right, it was a successful movie, but I didn't make much money from it, it paid for me to go back to school, it paid the mortgage, so to speak, well, literally it paid the mortgage on the house Daphne and I had bought, we were separated but not divorced, the money from the movie kept us afloat for a few years while I went back to school and started a new career, but in any case Adam couldn't let go of the idea that I had lots of money, you wrote *Catbirds*, he said to me, he said it all the time, you wrote *Catbirds*, you must have made big bucks on that, and every time he said it I told him no, no, it didn't work out that way, my former writing partner wrote the script, Jeremy and I, we had split up, it was complicated, anyway, I didn't get rich, I made some money but I didn't get rich, I went back to school, I stopped trying to write movie scripts, I went to school to become a therapist, anyway, I had written the short story but Jeremy turned it into a screenplay, and in the end it was very different from what I had written, it wasn't really about our family anymore, but it still had the title I had given it, *Catbirds*, even though it was a completely different story in the end the name remained the same, *Catbirds*, in the end the movie wasn't about a family exploding, it was more a coming-of-age story, it was very successful, and Adam believed I had made a great deal of money from it, I could never make him understand that I hadn't gotten rich from *Catbirds*, that I didn't have much money, because Daphne and I were separated, we had to pay for two households, and Muriel was in private school, it wasn't like I had money to put into some cockamamie scheme that Adam had come up with, I had told him a dozen times I wasn't wealthy, it was the opposite, I was close to broke, it was annoying when Adam insisted I must be rich, but I didn't really recognize, at the time, I mean, how deluded Adam was, yes, that was the word, deluded, I didn't understand what was happening to him

*Adam worked in the financial industry for more than ten years,
achieving many of his ambitions, but in later years he struggled
a little*, no, that isn't how to describe it, *but in later years,
unfortunately, he lost his license*, did they call it a license, are
there licenses to work on Wall Street, *he was barred from working
in the securities industry*, that was the way it was phrased, but
why bring that up, not that anyone will be there to hear it, still,
why bring it up, *unfortunately he suffered a significant business
reversal*, yes, that would be how to put it, *and in the aftermath
he struggled to find a satisfactory way of making a living, but he
remained ambitious*, yes he always had a scheme, he was always
offering advice, stock tips, in fact the very last time we got
together he had some scheme he was pushing at me, god what
a day that was, we met in Grand Central, at the bar at the top
of the marble staircase, and the waiter brought Adam a drink,
a vodka tonic, with a lemon wedge, not a lime wedge, which for
some reason set Adam off, a lemon wedge in a vodka tonic, he
said, who puts a lemon wedge in a vodka tonic, and he called
the waiter over to tell him that there was a lemon wedge in his
drink, as if it were a hair or a rat dropping in there, it was just
a lemon wedge, my god, what a perfect example of Adam's ill
temper, the slice of yellow fruit in his cocktail was an insult,
a provocation, he was practically ready to accost someone,
complain to the maître d', but the waiter made a show of servility,
brought us a free dish of olives, a free replacement drink,

the waiter knew what he was doing, he could see what he was
dealing with in Adam, Cipriani Dolci, that was the name of
the place, Adam had suggested it as a place to meet, he took
the train all the way into the city just to have drinks with
me at Cipriani Dolci in Grand Central, I was touched that
he would make the trip, it was brotherly of him, I had never
known him to make an effort like that to see me, or to see
anyone in the family, as far as I knew, and when he offered
to come into the city, I told him we could meet halfway, we
could meet in Stamford or even Westport, but he insisted on
coming all the way to the city, it wasn't a short trip, but he
wanted to meet in New York, and when I arrived at the bar
to meet him, he was sitting at one of the tables overlooking
the concourse, but he was facing away from the view, which
seemed strange, why would you face away from the sight, the
information booth in the center of the concourse, the famous
clock on top, the golden clock, that scene in *The Catcher in the
Rye*, and the night skyscape on the vaulted ceiling, he wasn't
looking at any of that, he was facing the wrong way, sitting at
a table, hunching over the table, he seemed too large for the
little table, the way he hung over it, and I thought for a minute
he was looking at a phone or a book, but no, he was just sitting
there, brooding, hunching, hulking, and I had a bad feeling,
before I actually spotted him at the table I had been feeling
optimistic, I was touched, even, that he would make the trip all
the way into the city, just to see me, but when I saw him there,
hunched at the table, facing away from the spectacle of Grand
Central, I realized I had read it wrong, something was off, and
immediately he made a scene about the lemon wedge, what a
thing to be upset about, and it turned out the only reason he
had wanted to get together was to sell me on something, he
wanted me to invest in a fund, I had no idea what it was, how

could he even be involved in something like that, I wondered, wasn't he barred from the financial industry, I wondered, but he was dismissive, oh, he said, let me worry about that, he said, let me be the one to worry about compliance, that was an enraging, patronizing thing to say, let me be the one to worry about compliance, I told him I had no money, which actually was true, but he refused to believe it, he asked me about *Catbirds*, I had told him already several times that I wrote the story but I didn't have anything to do with the script or the movie, and besides I wasn't a writer anymore, he could never be bothered to understand what I did for a living, he wondered if there was much money in being a shrink, and I said, Adam, I said, oh, please, let's not get into that, can we not get into that, but of course he couldn't be dissuaded, he had to press, it was his nature, so we got in an argument at the bar in Grand Central, under the dusky-aqua night sky painted across the vaulted ceiling, because of course I was not going to invest in some hedge fund that Adam was talking up, I didn't have any money for that, the only person in the family with money was Mom, she had inherited some money from her second husband, and then she married Carl, who was pretty well-off, so Mom had money, but she would not invest with Adam, she and Adam even as adults could not be in the same room together, I suppose the same could be said for me although I did try to see Adam periodically, but that was the time, that time at the bar in Grand Central, when Adam made a comment about Muriel, he wondered why Muriel did not particularly look like me, she looked like Jeremy, did I ever wonder, he asked, why my daughter looked so much like my former writing partner, Jeremy

When Daphne offered to fly east for the memorial service I told
her not to bother, but she insisted that she should come, he's
your older brother no matter what, she said, and she added,
a person's a person no matter how small, quoting Dr. Seuss, it
was an old joke, we had read the book to Muriel, *Horton Hears
a Who!*, a person's a person, no matter how small, and Muriel
had been very small, very delicate, we called her Little Muriel
Who, or Little Moohoo, and even as a young woman Muriel
remained small, and yes I always think that I am relatively
small, not very tall, pretty thin, taking after my mother, but
by contrast Jeremy, my writing partner, was large, he was big
and bluff, he had that confidence about him, a large man's
confidence, he had bluster, bluster and copper-colored curls,
you could see him in a crowd, he stood out, and Muriel had
reddish hair, nothing like Daphne or me, that was what Adam
was getting at, why did my daughter have red hair, and also
because Daphne had been Jeremy's girlfriend before she was
mine, so that was complicated, there was that backstory, and
then Daphne had reconnected with Jeremy, very complicated,
a stupid situation, maybe it was inevitable because Jeremy
had dated Daphne first, that was how I had met her, and at
the time I was single, and Jeremy was my best friend, so we
spent a fair amount of time as a threesome, not that kind of
threesome, we ate dinner together, we drove to San Diego
to see the underwater national park, we did things together,

the three of us, Jeremy and I would work together during
the day, and then the three of us would go out together at
night, Jeremy needed an audience, I guess, and at some point
I remember Daphne and I began to trade glances, not flirting,
just responding to Jeremy's absurd ego, he could be a buffoon,
claiming to know about wine, returning bottles, he did that a
couple times and we couldn't help it, Daphne and I looked at
one another and traded knowing glances, that was how a bond
was forged between us, exasperation with Jeremy, who, as it
turned out, was having an affair while he was seeing Daphne,
and I was the one who learned of it first, I kept quiet for a bit,
but Daphne figured it out soon after that, and then one thing
led to another, well, it was essentially instantaneous, the same
night she learned about Jeremy having an affair, she slept with
me, or I slept with her, however you phrase it, so Daphne ended
up with me, and Jeremy ended up with a new girlfriend, and
yet Jeremy and I kept writing together for years and years,
even though I had, if you looked at it in a certain way, stolen
his girlfriend from him, I had ended up marrying her, he had
dated Daphne before me, but anyway, the fact of the matter is
that he was the engine of our writing partnership, he was the
showman, he won us the jobs, and when we wrote together, that
was mostly him too, somehow we worked together for years
and years, and I can admit now that I didn't contribute much
to our scripts, but Jeremy often said, I couldn't do it without
you, pal, he had the movie-business way of speaking, he would
grab me by the neck with his enormous hands and massage
me roughly, why are you so tense, I can feel your tension, he
had huge, meaty hands, Jeremy was a big guy overall, a good
four or five inches taller than me, those big hands, freckled on
the back, he had freckles everywhere, the coppery hair, even
when he started losing his hair, even then his curly hair was

noticeable, it had a way of catching the light, and at some point we didn't seem to be getting any work, and Jeremy blamed me, I had lost my mojo, he said, or that's what he said at first, and later he got frustrated, he told me to shut up when we were in meetings, nothing I said was funny, he said, why did you say that thing about Greenpeace, he asked me that once, after a meeting, why did you say that thing about Greenpeace, and I told him I had thought it would be funny, and he said, Greenpeace is never funny, he said, obviously Greenpeace is never funny, he said, you're *trying*, I can see you *trying*, well, it was unpleasant, looking back on it I imagine it was because he felt guilty, he had started sleeping with Daphne again, or maybe it was just frustration, and when I found out, when Daphne admitted what had happened, I moved out, and that's not all, I turned my life upside down, as the saying goes, I moved out, I decided I was going to go back to school, I was going to become a therapist, it was all new, and I assumed Jeremy and Daphne would get married or at least get back together even if they didn't get married, but in fact it seemed like it was just a fling between them, although who ever really knows the truth of these things, but after a while Daphne and I repaired the relationship, it took years, the three years in school, two more getting my hours for licensing, it took a long time but I built a new life, we had to maintain good relations for Muriel, for Em, as we called her, Muriel had no freckles, she had coppery hair but no freckles, and she was delicate and small, bird-sized, small-framed like Daphne, like me, Little Muriel Who, Little Moohoo, I lived away from her most of her high school years, Daphne didn't even want me to move out when she had an affair with Jeremy, she didn't want me to but I did, I felt I had to, my pride was wounded, as the saying goes

But that was the reason I had finally cut off relations with Adam, I had put up with his bullying and his sour moods and his patronizing comments about my struggles to make a living, and also his feigned concern for my well-being, for years he had asked if Daphne's income was secure, given the situation with my career, which, by the way, I had made some money, Jeremy and I had sold scripts, not just optioned them but sold them, so we were already in the one-percent-luckiest group of writers in Hollywood, I told Adam that, I explained it to him, do you realize, I asked him, do you realize how tough it is to get a script sold, let alone two, plus we had been hired to do some rewrites, we weren't getting rich but we had each bought a house, Jeremy had a place in Mid-City, Daphne and I lived near the Santa Monica Airport, it was a modest place, Spanish style, walls the color of Band-Aids, tile floors that warmed in the sun, the private planes that flew in and out of the airport would buzz above us, just a hundred feet or so above us, it was comical, almost, although there had been a crash at one point, not that it damaged our house but it was sobering, in any case, I did explain to Adam that what I had accomplished, working with Jeremy, was not nothing, I don't remember what he said exactly, whatever, I think he said, whatever, that was the word he used, and then, I think he added, I don't know how the two of you can still be working together, given your *history*, yes, he said something about our history, Jeremy and my history,

the fact that Daphne had been Jeremy's girlfriend before I
started seeing her, and then Jeremy and Daphne had resumed
their relationship, Adam knew all this, I had told him about
it, I should have kept it to myself but I told him, and he said to
me, I told you she would try to destroy you, and it was true that
I felt destroyed, I felt destroyed by what Daphne and Jeremy
had done, but of course Adam wasn't talking about hearts and
feelings, he was talking about money, when he said she would
destroy me he had meant that Daphne would try to take all
my money, not that I had much money, he said that she would
try to destroy me basically because that was what happened in
his own marriage, and it was true that he didn't have nearly as
much money after he and Celeste were divorced, he went from
his mansion in Greenwich to a fairly modest condo in Norwalk,
I don't know what happened to the Greenwich mansion, did
Celeste keep it, I didn't really know, and meanwhile there
was some kind of lawsuit involving his work, there were civil
charges, from what I could understand there were judgments
against Adam that had practically bankrupted him, and the
civil suits kept coming, and he brought countersuits, for a
while after he got divorced he had the condo in Norwalk, it
was a nice place, it had a pool, he was alone but he wasn't
completely broke, he wasn't broke yet, it was a few years before
he lost the condo, too, and ended up in his apartment in the
Treadway building in Ogden, not far from the highway, you
could hear the trucks barreling down I-95, and it wasn't until
later, when I was dealing with his apartment and looking into
the particulars of his death, it wasn't until then that I realized
that, the last time I saw him, Adam hadn't been asking me
to invest in a hedge fund, he had been looking for a loan, he
wanted a handout, I just hadn't understood what he was saying
to me, because even though I knew Adam had been barred

from the securities industry, and I knew that he had lost his house and then his condo, I still couldn't quite understand that he would come to me for money, I couldn't imagine him as actually broke, not after all those years of him peacocking about his success in life, his degree from Yale, his positions on Wall Street, not that I ever really understood what he did, after listening to him boast about his five-bedroom mansion in what must be the richest suburb in the country, in the world, it just didn't occur to me that he was so broke that he would need a loan from me, and then there was the way he made the request, it didn't sound like he was asking for a loan, he made it sound like I would be investing in something he had dreamed up, and I didn't have any money, I really did not, I was still getting my practice started, I had gone back to school, Daphne and I were separated and I was strapped, why would I invest in some cockamamie scheme my brother was ranting about, how could he think I would be interested in a crazy scheme like that, so I told him no, of course I was not in any position to put money into a special fund, and that was when he made the crack about Muriel, suggesting that maybe she was Jeremy's daughter

Not that I hadn't thought of that once or twice on my own, Em's coppery hair, it really did remind me of Jeremy, not just the hair either, not that she really resembled Jeremy but on the other hand she didn't really look like Daphne or me, I don't know, I saw echoes of me in Em, she was slender, she laughed the way I laughed, we liked the same sorts of food, either way, if I had realized that what Adam had really needed was money, he needed a loan, he needed a grant of money outright, maybe it would have turned out differently, but I didn't realize it at the time, instead of lending him money I just stormed out of the bar at Grand Central, I left him sitting with his free dish of olives and a vodka tonic, the lemon wedge, the lime wedge, I left him sitting there alone at the little table under the twinkling lights of the vaulted ceiling, of course I stormed out, what choice had he left me, what did he expect of me, that I wouldn't be offended when he intimated that Muriel wasn't actually my biological daughter, of course I stormed out, and not only that, I didn't call him for several years, I cut him off, good riddance, I thought, I had never, quite honestly, liked Adam, and now I had no reason to pretend otherwise, and in fact I barely ever thought of him, only when someone asked me about my family, if I had any brothers or sisters, then I would think of him, I would answer, four brothers, even though Willie was dead so there were really only three of us, and even that was not quite accurate, not that I was lying but it was complicated, there was also our half brother, Terry, my father's son from his first marriage, but I rarely saw Terry when I was growing up, he had emotional issues, when he came to visit he tended to separate himself, I remember him curling up in the corner of the living room and reading, sitting there all day, maybe he was freaked out by Adam and Willie, or maybe it was all of us, he was accustomed to living alone with his mother in western Massachusetts, anyway, I rarely saw Terry, and when my father died I remember wondering about his lack of connection with Terry, his first son, wondering about how he could go, it seemed, months and months without speaking to him or even mentioning him, it reflected poorly on my father, I thought, but I didn't know the details, maybe Terry's mother didn't allow Terry to visit us except very rarely, but in any case my father was a distant person in general, he never engaged with us as boys, well, that's an exaggeration, but mainly I recall him sitting at a table on the porch in good weather, a huge stack of papers from work in front of him, while we ran around him, or charged through the screen door out to the backyard, it closed with an explosive bang, my mother, inside the house, probably talking on the phone in the little yellow room, talking on the phone and smoking a cigarette, calling out, *can you please not slam the screen door like that*, but my father, sitting right there, sitting not ten feet from the slamming screen door, never said anything about the noise, never told anyone to calm down, never asked anyone to use their indoor voice, but anyway, it was strange to think that of the four brothers, five if you count Terry, I was the only one who had had a child of his own, there had been five of us in our generation and the next generation there was just the one, Little Muriel, and in the end Adam and I weren't on speaking terms, I never called him once, not once, for more than three years, not after the incident at Cipriani Dolci in Grand Central, I had my own life to live, I was getting started in a new career, I was working through my long separation from Daphne, why did I need the unpleasantness of Adam in my life, but then the pandemic came and I thought about him, I didn't know exactly where he lived at that point, or I hadn't been there, but I had looked it up on Google Maps, I had Google-stalked him, it was a glum-looking apartment building across the street from a tire dealer, the grass in front of the building was thin and yellow, and it may have been a trick of the light but the windows of the building looked blotchy, I counted up to the fourth floor, I knew he lived on the fourth floor, Apartment 4H, and I wondered if one of those windows was his, honestly it looked like it might be an old-age home, an assisted-living facility, because there was an aluminum ramp running up to the front door, and, in the Google Street View photo of the building there happened to be an old woman sitting on a bench in front of the building, her face was blurred out but you could see that she had a walker pulled up in front of her, and next to her was someone who seemed to be wearing scrubs, probably a home health aide, anyway, I thought of Adam alone there, having fallen so far from his grand beginnings, alone and isolated, I assumed he was basically alone and isolated, and I was mostly right about that, he was basically alone in his little apartment in Ogden, close to the highway, maybe twenty minutes from the campus of Yale University, which had been his great achievement in life, he was all alone, he was a mean and angry man but he was my brother and I worried about him, alone during the lockdown, and so even though I didn't want to do it I picked up the phone and called him

I glanced at my watch and wondered how much longer it would be before Daphne arrived, she had flown in on the red-eye, the arrival was delayed for some reason but she said she thought she would still make it to the memorial on time, although you could never be sure about the traffic, still, there was nobody in the meeting room yet, and I gave in to a brief spasm of panic and looked at my phone, had I gotten the hour wrong, or maybe even the day, no, besides, I had seen the sign on the easel outside the door, *Memorial for Adam Green, 11 a.m., June 14, 2022*, I was on time, I was early, I had gotten there early on purpose, knowing that Mom would not arrive until the last moment, most likely, the animosity between them had lasted Adam's whole life so why wouldn't it linger for years after he died, after all she had already lost one son, Willie, Willie who was so delicate, that death led to the end of her marriage to Dad, even though Dad was sick and needed Mom's help, even so she left, Willie's death was like a bomb going off, but this was Adam's funeral, Adam's memorial service, not Willie's, I still had not composed my eulogy for Adam, although at least I had the starting point, but it would have been helpful to have Daphne there, she had always been a good editor, but her flight was delayed, she would still make it, Muriel was driving, Em, Little Moohoo, who seemed too small to drive even now that she was a sophomore in college, but no, Adam's eulogy, *Adam worked in the financial industry for more than ten*

years, achieving many of his ambitions, unfortunately he suffered a significant business reversal, and in the aftermath he struggled to find a satisfactory way of making a living, but he remained ambitious, and then what, what was there to say about his last years, at that point admittedly I had cut him off, the comments about Muriel stung, I never forgot them, and for three years I didn't call him or arrange to see him, I didn't let him know when I was back east, I would fly into JFK, rent a car, and blow right through Connecticut, passing within a mile of his apartment, less, but then I called him, it was the lockdown, I was worried about him, and I was right, as it turned out, I was right to be worried about him, I called him up and he seemed weirdly guarded, for instance he told me he thought he had Covid the day I called, which frightened me to hear, calling from California, but when I asked why he thought he had Covid, he said something about having vomited all afternoon the day before, which didn't sound like Covid to me, and then he said, I should probably go to the supermarket, and I asked if he could drive, but he said he would take a bus, oh, no, I said, if you're sick, please don't take the bus, so he said, or a friend could take me, and remembering that conversation, as I sat in the library meeting room, waiting for the memorial service to begin, I wondered if the friend was Julia, the woman who had sent him a card that I found in his bureau after he died, in the same drawer with the gun, a note from a woman, a gun, and a couple dozen carefully folded polo shirts, size XXL, he was up to XXL by the end I guess, anyway, when we spoke that last time, he seemed off, I should have done something more, but he was, in my mind, still Adam, and he hadn't seemed to care much that I had reached out, and besides the call was so strange, with him sounding perfectly healthy but also suggesting that he had Covid, and that he had vomited all afternoon the day before, and after a few minutes of disjointed conversation I said something insincere, I said, okay, Adam, be well, we'll talk again soon, well, that wasn't insincere exactly, but what I really meant was that I wanted to get off the phone, I rushed to end our conversation because it was so painful to talk to him in that state, he seemed slightly dazed, I would say, and I wanted to end the conversation and get back to my own life, and that was the last time I spoke to him

Well, he *was* dazed during that last conversation, it turned out, because he was taking a variety of sleeping pills, which I discovered when I was cleaning out his apartment after he died, there were dozens of bottles of prescription meds in his bathroom cabinet and in a kitchen cupboard and in the drawer of his bedside table, that was a sad drawer, it was full of his old business cards, from years ago, cards that he kept for no good reason, obviously he couldn't bring himself to get rid of them, and amid the old business cards and loose pens and coins and rubber bands were two orange-pink medication bottles, one was Lunesta and one was for Klonopin, that was serious, but when I looked more closely at the bottles I saw that they weren't made out to Adam but to someone named Julia Slotkin, and I assumed that this Julia Slotkin was the same Julia who had sent Adam the card that I found in his shirt drawer, the shirt-and-pistol drawer I mean, and when I checked the names on the pill bottles I found in the bathroom and the kitchen, several of them were made out to Julia Slotkin as well, and they were all relatively recent, I wasn't sure what it meant, but looking at the different meds, most of them were antidepressants or antipsychotics or sleep aids, I recalled the last conversation I had with Adam, at the beginning of the Covid lockdown, and remembered his weirdly dazed tone, he didn't sound like himself, and no wonder, if he was taking Lexapro or Lunesta or Ativan or Klonopin or any of the other meds I found in his apartment, although it was possible, I thought, that *Julia* was taking these drugs, I realized, and I picked up my phone and looked up Julia Slotkin in Ogden, and I found her, not in Ogden but the next town over, in Milford, but I didn't call her at first, first I collected all the bottles and looked at them, spread out on the narrow counter of Adam's little kitchen in the Treadway building, the toxicology report on Adam's postmortem showed antidepressants in his system, also alcohol, although it said moderate amounts, Adam had moderate amounts of antidepressants and alcohol in his body when he died, when he drowned, and here were antidepressants, and in one of the cabinets in the kitchen were two bottles of vodka, that was the only liquor in the house, one open bottle of vodka and one yet to be opened, there were also bottles of beer in the fridge, but I had bought those, Evan and I were drinking beers as we cleared out Adam's belongings, Evan was being careless, he didn't care much what happened to Adam's stuff, he wanted to pitch it in a dumpster, or burn it, but I kept finding things, the gun in the drawer, the note from Julia, the bottles of antidepressants and sleeping pills, I called for Evan to come look, look at all these meds, and he looked at the bottles irritably and said, yes, so what, he said, we already knew that Adam had antidepressants in his system, that's what the police report said, and he was right, yes, here was the proof, Adam had been a little drunk, a little zonked on some pills, maybe he was wandering around one evening and simply fell into the canal, although it didn't sound like Adam, he never wandered, he wasn't someone who strolled around in the evenings, or I didn't imagine that he would do that, for instance I could remember him walking up and down our block very purposefully one Christmas Day, talking loudly into a cell phone, and he said into the cell phone, he hollered, I guess you

could say, he hollered, I guess I'll be the asshole, because guess
what, he hollered, I don't mind being the asshole, that was what
I heard him say as he marched up and down the street in front
of our house, he was only one year out of college at that point
and already working on Wall Street, he was making a huge
amount of money, it seemed to me, I was still a college student,
and he was striding around, looking very cocky, wearing a dark
wool overcoat, and he spoke into the phone to someone about
being an asshole, loud enough for everyone on the street to hear
him, and I thought at the time, I actually thought, well, no
one on this street will be surprised to hear Adam admitting to
being an asshole, anyone who has lived on this street near us for
the last twenty years will know that this is Adam being Adam,
just in a new guise, a businessman's guise, a Wall Street banker's
guise, but the point is that Adam didn't stroll, he wouldn't have
gone out for a stroll and fallen into a canal, and the police were
no help, once Adam had been identified, they didn't really
care why Adam was in the canal, they had other fish to fry,
so to speak, they were spraying protesters with tear gas, Black
Lives Matter, even in a little town like Ogden for some reason
they were spraying people with tear gas, although some of the
marchers had thrown rocks at shopwindows, anyway, the police
weren't interested in Adam's case, they didn't even call it a case,
Detective Manfredi snorted, just a little, when I referred to it
as a case, he had no patience for me at the moment, he might
be a decent guy under other circumstances, I thought, but in
the moment, Covid lockdowns, hospitals filled up with sick
people, EMTs getting sick, marches, tear gas, he didn't think
there were any unanswered questions about Adam

Some of you may be wondering about the circumstances of Adam's death, and while we'll never have all the answers, we do know some things, we know that he was in poor health, he was diabetic, he may have been confused and wandered away from his apartment on the night of May 12, and it seems like he accidentally fell in the water near his home, well, not as close to his home as I had thought originally, I had wandered around his neighborhood, down to the waterfront, empty lots, abandoned warehouses, but there was a kind of marina there, an inlet off the river, the closest waterfront to his apartment, so I went there thinking I should see where he died, I assumed it was there, near his apartment, that he had been found in the water, face down, but when I got there I was surprised, it was fenced off, he would have had to climb over a chain-link fence, I didn't imagine he could have done it, maybe back in the day when he was a football player, but by the time he was in his late forties he was too heavy for that, I couldn't imagine him scaling a fence like that, so I backtracked and followed the next street down to the water, and this location seemed more likely, there was just a low fence, a railing, basically, and all along the perimeter were wooden pilings, that was what had banged up Adam's face, according to Detective Manfredi, Adam's body had bumped and scraped against the pilings, so this all made sense, and I could imagine Adam coming to this low railing and maybe stepping over it, maneuvering his heavy body over the railing, why, why would

he do that, maybe he was confused, maybe he was doped up on
the drugs I had found in his apartment, maybe he just climbed
over the railing in a drug haze, it would be easy enough to do,
I tried it myself, yes, I could easily lift my leg over the railing,
I climbed right over, no problem, and looked down into the
water, it was greenish brown, it was a hot day, and down below
me, there was a man sleeping in an inflatable boat, a little
pontoon boat with an outboard motor, lying motionless below
me, a baseball cap pulled over his face, and I think I must
have made a sound, I was surprised, I was taken aback to see
someone down there, he was heavyset, like Adam, his shirt was
riding up his belly, I could see his hairy belly and I thought, I
was confused, I thought, my god, it's Adam, although of course
I knew it wasn't Adam, it was a momentary confusion, just as
Adam, on the night that he died, might have had a moment of
confusion, having for some reason climbed over the fence and
fallen in the water, but I was surprised to see someone down
there and I made a little gasp, loud enough that the man in the
boat below me stirred, he pushed back his cap to peer up at
me and narrowed his eyes in the sun, and I asked for his help, I
asked if he had heard anything about the man who died in the
water here recently, had he heard about that, and he nodded,
although he didn't say anything for a moment, and then he said,
that wasn't here, that guy didn't die here, and I was surprised,
I was sure this must be the place, the low fence, the pilings,
close to Adam's apartment, but the man in the boat said no,
it was over there, and he gestured with his left hand, pointing
toward the highway, over by the Sunrise Marina, he said, and he
squinted at me a little, he had a very red face, not from sunburn
I mean, he had brown skin but his face was very red, I wondered
if I had unnerved him by asking if he knew anything about a
dead man in the water, that would be unnerving, to be woken

from a nap in a little boat and be asked about a dead man in the water, so I told him that it had been my brother, the man who died was my brother, I said, which seemed to touch the man in the boat, he sat up a little, he removed his baseball cap and held it to his chest, it was a sign of distress and respect, and he said, I'm sorry, mister, he called me mister, he had an accent of some sort, I couldn't place it, and he said, mister, if you want, I know the guy who found him, who found your brother, yeah, he said, he works over at the marina there, at Murphy's, the gas dock, you know, his name is João, João was the one who found him, you go there and ask for João, and I thanked him, I wanted to ask his name but I didn't want to unnerve him any more than I already had, I didn't want to make his face turn any redder, I thanked him and hoped he didn't have dangerous hypertension, he was overweight, like Adam had been, and he looked to be about Adam's age, Adam's age before he died, no wonder I had confused him for Adam briefly, I found myself wishing the man would go to the doctor, he had been so thoughtful, removing his cap and sitting up when he heard that my brother had died, so I told him I was trying to find out more about my brother's death, I told him that the police weren't very helpful, and he seemed to understand, he was sympathetic to me, he wasn't surprised to hear that the police hadn't been helpful, and he told me again to go to Murphy's at the Sunrise Marina and ask for João

So I went looking for João, and the Sunrise Marina wasn't far, just a few blocks up from Adam's apartment, the Treadway apartment house, Adam could have walked it easily, even if drugged up he could have walked it, and when I came to the marina, it was nicer than I expected, that is, it was still rundown, the water was dirty and oily, but it wasn't fenced off, you could walk right up to the piers and the water's edge, and there were party boats there, shuttered for the pandemic I guess, Hi-Rolla Fishing Trips, Melinda Q Sport Fish, Sweet Blues, but it wasn't just a wasteland, like the inlets farther up, it was a lively place, or it would have been if not for the pandemic, there was a bulletin board by the gas pump at Murphy's, advertisements for fishing trips and boat services, and at the window I asked if João was around and the man inside told me to look out back, where I found a heavyset guy seated on a plastic crate cracking peanuts on his lap, he wasn't wearing a face mask but I kept mine on, there were seagulls flapping around, waiting to see if the man might drop a peanut, and I hesitated, he was so burly, his tattooed arms were forbidding, but I approached him after a moment and told him I was looking for João, and he said that was who he was, he was João, at first he didn't seem to want to talk, he ate his peanuts and avoided my eyes, but I explained who I was, I told him I was Adam's brother, I tried to make him understand that all I wanted was to see the place where Adam's body had been found, and he sat there on his milk-crate

stool, shaking his head, muttering to himself, he had a kind
of a speech impediment, he was soft-spoken despite his size,
and for some reason he told me about one of the gulls hopping
around the tarmac in front of him, he called one of the gulls
Crazy Sandro, Crazy Sandro, you want a peanut, he muttered,
but he didn't throw the bird a treat, he only cracked another
nut, ate it, and let the shells flutter to the pavement between
his knees, I didn't know what to make of him, he didn't seem
to want to look me in the face, I said, again, the drowned man
was my brother, I said, I just want to have a look at where he
died, I just want to see where it was, was it here, but it seemed
like João wasn't even paying attention to me, he was watching
one of the gulls, the one he called Crazy Sandro, and I could
see there was something wrong with the bird, its wing didn't
fold up properly, it had a jerky way of moving, and João said
to the bird, you got a shock, and finally to me João said, he got
electric shock, his feathers burnt, he can't fly right, something
like that, it was hard to understand him, he pronounced the
words in a way I could barely make out, and I had to repeat
it all back to him, but then I understood, I understood why
he was telling me about the seagull, he was saying that Crazy
Sandro had been there when Adam died, that was what João
was telling me, because he couldn't fly, really, Crazy Sandro
had a hiding place near the gas pump, he didn't leave this dock,
so he was there the night that Adam died, João grunted and
pointed at the bird, it was as if he was saying, you see, you see,
the bird was the one who really knew what happened, the bird
was there, the bird saw it all, and then João pushed himself up
and limped away, toward the water's edge, and he looked across
the canal and pointed at one of the pilings, see, he said, see
that light, he said, he was floating under the light, it was early,
like night, you know, the light was on, he was float in the light,

that's where he was, and the two of us, João and I, stared across the oily water at the place where he had found Adam's body, over there, I said, and João nodded, I could see he was sad, I think he was sad to look at the place that he had seen Adam, he gestured with his arms to show the way Adam was floating, so I said, he was floating face down, and he nodded again, and he said, I see him, I call the police, that's all I know, okay, and he turned and walked back toward his milk carton, calling out to the bird, Crazy Sandro, he said, I give you a peanut this time, and the malformed bird hopped around nervously, I wondered if the bird really had been there, had it been there to see Adam topple into the water, did it watch as Adam died there, face down in the turbid water, maybe there had been dozens of gulls wheeling over the canal as Adam fell in, banging his head, who knows, maybe he was pushed, the cops said no, he banged his head on a piling, he scraped his face in the water, his wallet could have fallen out, who knows, and I stood there by the water for a while, feeling the weight of the sun on my head, the bald spot at the back of my head, Adam had it too, we were nothing alike but our hair had thinned the same way, you could see a little of his scalp at the back, my hair was the same way now, the two of us losing our hair the same way, I could imagine the sun coming up that morning, the morning he died, would it have burned the skin, even if he was already dead, who knows, he was dead, he was face down, he drowned, there were drugs in his system but he drowned, there was no foul play, that's what Detective Manfredi said, that was the phrase he used, no foul play, but at least now I had seen the place where Adam had died, it was sad but at least now I knew exactly where he had died, I had been to the place, I had seen the water, and I hurried back to the Treadway, to Adam's apartment, and Evan was inside, still cleaning out the apartment, bagging up Adam's belongings to be donated to Goodwill, he didn't want any of Adam's belongings, neither did I, it was hard to understand how Adam, who had once been so rich, could have ended up with nothing, I let myself into the apartment and I told Evan I had found the canal where Adam had died, I had seen the place his body was found, I offered to take Evan there, so he could see it too, so he could see where Adam had been found, but he said no, he said, no, I have no interest in that

About Adam's health, I should say a few words, he had diabetes, but some of us were less aware that he had struggled in his later years with mental illness, well, I suppose you could say he was mentally ill, mentally unstable, all his life, but I only understood that in retrospect, or no, it didn't occur to me to think of his behavior that way, it was just Adam, that was how I thought of it, Angry Adam, that was another nickname Evan had for him, Angry Adam, also he called him Adam Ant, and Klondike, that was the one that he came up with for Adam once Adam was out of the house, Klondike, I don't know where he got that, but somehow it fit Adam, I could imagine Adam prospecting in the gold rush, he was money-hungry like the old prospectors, he would stop at nothing if there was money in it for him, at some point it was all he thought about, once he was in college all he could talk about was money, markets, stocks, bonds, I didn't know what he was talking about most of the time, but he was already making a lot of money from summer jobs on Wall Street, he called it an internship but he made thousands of dollars, he bought expensive clothing, he was dressing the part even when he was nineteen or twenty, he strode around on the street in front of our house talking on his cell phone, a Motorola flip phone it was, who he was talking with, I don't know, why would a Wall Street firm need to talk to its interns on a weekend, the conversations went so long that the phone grew too hot to touch, feel this, he said, holding the phone out to me when he was done talking, feel it, he said, it's practically burning up, and he touched the phone to my cheek and it was just as he said, it was as if the phone had been heated over an open flame, like a hot poker, that was how much he cared about his job and money and stocks, he would hold a phone so hot to his cheek it might have scarred him, it might have burst into flame, and that was when he was still in college, imagine him later, after he graduated, he was working for some firm, making more money than my father, *his* father, at the age of twenty-one or twenty-two he was making more money than our father, and he had an apartment in downtown Manhattan, we all visited one Saturday, and he took us to dinner, a steak house, and in the middle of the meal he had to take a call, because he always took the call, those were the days when people spoke endlessly on cell phones, it's not like that anymore, but in those days you always took the call, and he answered and ducked away from the table and my mother helped my father cut his meat, the Huntington's was really getting in his way now, he was unsteady on his feet, and my mother had to cut up my father's meals for him, if it was steak or chicken, he couldn't manage a knife, still, he would last another five years, longer than his marriage as it turned out, they hung on for a few years after Willie died, they made it to the point when Evan went to college, that visit to Adam in Manhattan, that was one of the last things we ever did as a family, as a whole family, Willie's death killed the marriage, choked it off, after Willie died my mother spent less time at home, most days she drove over to her sister's house the next town over, that's where she said she was going, the family got very quiet then, I don't remember my parents talking much, they didn't talk with me, they didn't talk with each other, I was away at college, Evan was the last one left at home, Mom and Dad only talked to him, he was the baby of the family, and once Willie and Adam and I were gone, they talked with Evan, individually, my mother talked with him and my father talked with him, but they didn't really talk with each other, just Evan, and pretty soon after Evan went away to school my mother moved out, and my father couldn't negotiate the house by himself and he moved to an apartment just outside New Haven, and just like that the family was done, although somehow Evan remained close with both Mom and Dad, I suppose because he was the youngest, he was separate, somehow, from Adam and Willie and me, we came in a rush, he was almost five years later than us, Adam and Willie and I were always fighting, fighting for attention, fighting just to fight, and Evan was too small to take part, and Mom and Dad never seemed to pay much attention to the fighting, well, every once in a while Mom would seem to notice, she would scream up the stairs, scream from the kitchen, scream from the little yellow room behind the kitchen, stop it, she would scream, would you boys just stop it, you're driving me crazy, but she didn't do anything about the fighting, the crashing, the falling down the stairs, once Adam pushed me down the stairs, trying to ram past me, but for some reason I didn't want to move out of his way that one time, I stood my ground, but he was bigger and heavier and two years older and the force of his chest against my back was enough to knock me off my feet, and I fell down the stairs, practically the whole flight of stairs, the sound of my falling got my mother's attention, she called out from the kitchen, don't break the stairs, just don't do it, and it turned out I had sprained my wrist and for the next two weeks I had to write with my left hand, that was thanks to Adam, but I didn't tattle, I didn't complain to Mom or Dad, what was the point, she was on the phone in the little yellow room, Dad was at work or maybe working out on the porch,

where he never seemed to hear anything around him, he spread
out his piles of paper on the porch and sat there in deep
thought, what was he doing, I have no idea, he worked for a
small accounting firm, why did he have so much paperwork,
it made no sense, but he worked on the porch, or in the
sunroom by the porch when it was too chilly, he worked out
there for maybe nine months of the year, on weekends I mean,
and in the winter he worked on a folding card table in the
corner of his bedroom, and yet for all his time and focus on
the job, he didn't seem to make a great deal of money, or at
least it wasn't much in comparison to what Adam earned at
his first job on Wall Street after graduation, when my father
heard what Adam's salary and bonus were, he took off his
glasses and rubbed the bridge of his nose, and finally he said,
I'm proud of you, Adam, you're already outearning me, and I
detested Adam right then, I detested him for surpassing my
father, who was in the mid-stages of Huntington's by then, he
could still get around, he could work, he could do everything,
but he seemed weak, his voice was off, I hated Adam then, I
wondered why he couldn't have kept his salary to himself, he
must have known, or at least he must have guessed, that Dad
didn't make as much as he did, he could have said nothing, he
could have lied and said he made less, but that was Adam, that
was his competitive nature, and his hunger for money, money
was the only thing that seemed to satisfy him, he liked to spend
it, he liked expensive clothes, he bought a huge wardrobe when
he was in his twenties, a cashmere coat, a scarf that was silk
on one side and merino wool on the other, his shoes looked
like nothing to me, but he told me they had cost five hundred
simoleons, that was what he said, five hundred simoleons, these
are five-hundred-dollar shoes, he said, gesturing at them with
both hands, I remember he looked like he was doing some kind

of dance, five hundred bucks, that was a huge amount of money back then, and he told me that he had upgraded from shoes that cost three hundred and fifty dollars, and the price difference was worth it, one hundred percent, he said, and I wonder now if he was crazy all along, was he crazy as a boy, shouting *stampede* as he ran down the stairs, so intent on being first that he would just run over his brother, knock his brother, *me*, down the steps, spraining my wrist, was he crazy then, or what about when he was in his twenties, and buying cashmere coats and five-hundred-dollar shoes, was he crazy then or just a Wall Street bro, I think he must have been crazy all along, we all assumed Adam was just hypercompetitive, we assumed he was selfish, we assumed he resented Willie and me for being so close in age to him, for crowding him out of the family somehow, we assumed that he had faults, but now I think it was just his mental illness emerging, like a chick's beak breaking through an egg, there was something coming out but we just didn't see it, and even in his thirties and his early forties, I thought his run of bad luck was just a result of his competitiveness getting out of control, it led him into fights at work and with neighbors and local governments, and then lawsuits and bankruptcy and more lawsuits after that, and all along I just thought, if he could just tone it down a little, I didn't think he was crazy, I thought he was too intense, I didn't consider the possibility that he was actually mentally ill, but I think he must have been all along, right from the beginning

I heard a sound behind me in the Amory Public Library's meeting room, and I turned around, and saw a man about my age in the doorway, he had cleared his throat to get my attention, and at that point I knew I would have to go back, I couldn't sit in the front row any longer, I had to go back, I had to stand by the door and greet mourners, or guests, there really wouldn't be any mourners, I thought, well, there might be one, I wasn't sure if Julia Slotkin would be coming to the service or not, but whether or not anyone was truly mourning Adam, I stood up and walked back to the doorway, and the guy turned out to be a high school classmate of Adam's, I didn't recognize his name, but they had played football together, and I nodded and pretended to recall him after a moment, and thanked him for coming, and for some reason I apologized for the small crowd, if that was the right way to describe a room with two people in it, a small crowd, but he said some of Adam's high school buddies would be there in a minute, high school buddies was what he called them, it was a phrase I wouldn't have associated with Adam, I'm not sure why, buddies, high school buddies, it just didn't sound like Adam, not what I remembered of him, he had been so diligent, determined to get into an Ivy League school, especially Yale, Yale cast a kind of shadow over that whole area of Connecticut, it was almost as if that area had no reason to exist if not for Yale, as if we were all in service of the school, and in a way we really were, my family was, because my father's accounting firm, the accounting firm where he worked, it wasn't his accounting firm, he just worked there, in any case, his firm's main client was Yale, they did some kind of work for Yale, so our family circled like a tiny moon around the university, and every year several kids in our town went to Yale, there were connections, faculty members, that kind of thing, the top student at our town high school almost always went to Yale, it was a tradition, you could say, Adam was aware of that tradition, it was what drove him, maybe that was why I was surprised to hear his classmate refer to high school buddies, because Adam had struck me as humorlessly determined, even in high school, it didn't seem like he had time for buddies, but then again he did move around the school in a pack of football players, a group of big boys walking confidently down the halls, they weren't bullies, exactly, but people gave them room, they were big and strong, they looked like adults, some of them had beards and mustaches, that's just how it goes in high school, there are some kids who still look like children, and others who seem like grown men, Adam wished he had more of a mannish appearance, but his beard was still wispy in high school, I remember him peering at himself in the bathroom mirror, shaving what little stubble he had, he used to affect a deeper, growly voice to make himself seem older and, I suppose, tougher, I don't know that he ever grew a beard, when I grew one he made fun of it, are you trying to look like Sigmund Freud, he said, now that you're a shrink you've grown a beard, he observed, and I disliked him for that, I didn't like being called a shrink, I had gone back to school to become a family therapist, I worked mostly with children, it was so much better than the years I had spent trying to be a screenwriter, or being a screenwriter, working with Jeremy on screenplays, I was happier as a therapist, I was a good therapist, but Adam could never believe that, for years he asked about the movie *Catbirds*, I wrote the story that Jeremy turned into the screenplay, I wonder if Adam was jealous that I was associated with that movie, certainly he never could seem to get off the subject, how much money did I make from the movie, why would I walk away from that, money and power and prestige, that's what Adam cared about, and that was why I didn't think of him as having buddies, even in high school his focus had been to get the money, get power, get prestige, money, money, money, he had no time for buddies, or of course he did, of course he had time to make friends, he had friends in high school, I just didn't think of him that way, but I was having trouble knowing what to say to this first guest, this first mourner, Adam's high school buddy, it was difficult to know how to act, it had been two years since Adam's death, first there was the pandemic and no one wanted to have a service that year, and then somehow another year went by, and the reason, let's be honest, was that no one mourned Adam, no one in the family mourned him, in all honesty none of us really mourned him, we didn't wish him dead, exactly, but we didn't truly mind that he was gone, honestly, we didn't truly mind, I had to admit that to myself, that I didn't miss him, that I hadn't liked him, for some reason I had a hard time thinking that of myself, but Evan, well, Evan had no qualms about it, or he seemed to have no qualms about it, just a few weeks after Adam had died, while he and I were cleaning up Adam's apartment, Evan was already perfectly comfortable speaking ill of Adam, he called him a prick, I remember, which upset me somehow, it might have been hypocritical of me but I didn't like that Evan called Adam a prick so soon after Adam died, I didn't like him saying it out loud, I knew he felt that way,

I knew he had always felt that way, I felt that way too, but it seemed cruel to speak ill of the dead that way, and even now, two years later, when I asked Evan if he wanted to speak at the service, he laughed, he actually laughed, and said, why would I want to speak at Adam's funeral

I was still assembling my thoughts, I admitted to Adam's friend, Adam's high school buddy, I had already forgotten his name, I'm still putting the finishing touches on my eulogy, so if you would just have a seat, but then two more people arrived at the door, two more high school buddies, I learned, and I had to shake hands again, and one of the new pair seemed to be confused, he said, didn't Adam's brother, and his voice trailed off, and I guessed he must have been recalling something about Willie, that was what he must have been thinking, because he flushed and looked down and muttered, I was thinking of something else, he said, and the three of them went quiet and stared at their feet, and I noticed then that they weren't very large, these friends of Adam's, these high school football players, they weren't that much larger than me, a couple of them were on the beefy side, nothing special, not the way Adam had become, no, they were just a little beefy, but in any case they were essentially my size, not the way I remembered them in high school, not the way I remembered Adam, rolling down the halls in a confident group, *stampede*, of course I always heard that word in my head when I thought of it, and I said it out loud, *stampede*, I said, *stampede*, and I asked Adam's football buddies if they remembered Adam saying that, *stampede*, did they remember him saying that, and they shuffled a little, but no one seemed to remember it really, I think I remember that, one of them said, he said it in a way that it was obvious that he didn't remember at all, he was only being agreeable, and I wondered, was it possible that I remembered it all wrong, maybe Adam had not said *stampede* as often as I recalled, maybe I misremembered, because here were these grown men who were hardly more than my own size, maybe a little heavier than me, maybe an inch taller than me, but basically normal size, not the way I had remembered the high school football players, and I wondered if Adam had really just been normal size as well, after all, he wasn't really big enough or athletic enough to play college football, he had joined the college team as a walk-on, he was never a starting player in college, maybe he had just been a basically normal size all along, maybe I only remembered him as being bigger than me, I wondered how many other ways I might have misremembered him, he seemed so large and threatening in my memory

I'm Randy Green, thank you for joining my family today to remember Adam, my older brother, who grew up here in Amory, it was a small town, we led a small-town life, my parents and my brothers, we lived on Clinton Avenue, near Short Park, that was what we called it, we called it Short Park, that wasn't the actual name, we called it that because there was another park in town called Long Park, *and the house backed up on a little park, a wooded park, we used to run out our back door into the park, where we caught fireflies and we trapped frogs in the creek,* I didn't like that we kept the animals in jars and cardboard boxes, but Adam told me to shut up, he didn't go so far as to torture them, but he kept them in there too long, I cried for them being trapped in there, and Adam would become exasperated, I'm going to let them out soon, he said, they'll be fine, *there were four of us boys, Adam was the oldest, then Willie, then me, we were born in less than three years, three of us all together in a lump, and then, five years later, came Evan, the baby of the family, and Adam, as the oldest, was always the boss and the captain,* he always called shotgun, he had a gift for calling shotgun before it occurred to anyone else, he called shotgun the moment he stepped outside, that was his competitive streak, *anyone who knew Adam when he was growing up here in Amory will remember how competitive he was, I think his greatest disappointment was that he fell short of being the class valedictorian,* he had no special gifts, just a hunger for achievement, which turned into a hunger for money and prestige, but hunger like that is a gift too, isn't it, hunger, he had the gift of hunger, *he ended up as the salutatorian, the number two student in school, an honor for sure, he gave the introductory remarks at his graduation,* but for someone as hungry as Adam, finishing number two was as good as failure, and I remember he seemed deflated after the graduation ceremony, he trudged back to the car, and for once I beat him to it by calling shotgun in the school parking lot, and he stared at me darkly and said, why are you such a douchebag, *and after graduation he attended Yale, he was always proud of his association with the university, and it opened doors for him almost immediately, for instance he had a well-paid internship in New York after his freshman year, when the rest of us were mowing lawns for money, or flipping burgers, Adam was already wearing a suit,* working as an assistant on a trading desk, none of us really knew what he was up to down in New York, even my father, who was an accountant and might have understood, even he didn't really follow what Adam's job was, but we all knew he was making plenty of money, he's soulless, my mother said, she called him soulless, not to his face but she said it to her sister, talking to her on the phone, smoking and talking in the little yellow room, or maybe I didn't remember that correctly, maybe she said his work was soulless, I'm not sure, she didn't like us boys hanging around the kitchen, eavesdropping on her endless conversations with her sister, so I don't know for sure what she was saying, but I remember her using the word soulless in reference to Adam, although again maybe it wasn't about Adam at all, maybe it was my father she was referring to, I think Willie had already died, he was dead, I don't know why she would have said Willie was soulless, it wouldn't make sense, presumably it was Adam, but it might have been my father, now that I think of it, he wasn't really sick yet, I mean he wasn't really symptomatic, his voice was thicker, his handwriting got slightly larger and began sloping to the side, I remember noticing that and pointing it out to him but he didn't seem to mind, so what if his handwriting was getting worse, he said, practically everything was on computers these days, but he also was dropping things, papers, keys, dishes, he broke dishes regularly, they slipped from his fingers, Rafe, my mother said, exasperated, and he said, I think I must be getting old, and it was true, he was older than Mom, he had been fairly old when he married Mom, he was in his late thirties by then, he had already been married once, and had a son from that marriage

Terry, Dad's first son by his first wife, grew up to be an odd, childlike man, even in his fifties he seemed like a boy, unfinished, he was on the spectrum, he told me once, when I visited him in Chicago, why did I visit him, I don't know, I just made a point of visiting him, just twice, we were half brothers, I wanted the connection, the first time I visited him he told me he had been diagnosed as being on the autism spectrum, which was a satisfying discovery for him, he told me, because it explained why he had so much trouble understanding the ways other humans behaved and expected him to behave, and as it happened his wife, too, was on the spectrum, he told me, but I had always known that he was different, somehow, when I reached out to him to introduce myself as an adult, I was in my thirties by then, his reaction was strangely flat, that's nice, he said, and when I asked if he would like to get together, as I happened to be in Chicago for work, he said, yes, and that was all, I waited on the phone for him to say something more, but all he said was yes, and after a long silence I realized that was all he was going to say so I suggested a time to meet and he said, yes, again, that was all, so even from the first phone call with him I could tell, or I assumed, that there was something off about him, he was childlike and sweet in person, very nice, we went to a dog park together and watched his dog dig an enormous hole in the dirt, I was worried the dog might try to tunnel out, dig under the fence of the dog park, but Terry said that was just

what his dog liked to do, he didn't run around with the other
dogs, he just liked to dig holes, so he let him dig a new hole each
time they visited the park, and I saw it was true, the dog had
dug an entire archipelago of holes, archipelago, I don't know
how that word came to mind, anyway, it was an archipelago of
holes along one end of the park, the dog was essentially ruining
the park, I felt embarrassed for some reason, I could see other
dog owners were keeping an eye on us, I wanted to leave, but
Terry said the dog wasn't finished yet, he liked to dig a deep,
large hole, and so we waited on a bench in the shade while the
dog scraped away at his hole, the dirt flying up over the lip of
the hole, you couldn't even see the dog after a while, just the
dirt flying up, and at some point the dog was done, there was
dirt everywhere, and the other dogs stayed away, and we put
the dog's leash on without saying anything, Terry didn't say
good dog, or come here, he just put on the leash and walked
out of the park, that was my first visit with Terry, my older
half brother that I had never really known as a boy, Terry said
to me when I said goodbye, it's nice to meet you

I would not bring up Terry at Adam's memorial service, I thought, watching as more guests came through the doors at the back of the meeting room at the Amory Public Library, what was the point of mentioning Terry now, he was hardly even mentioned when we were growing up, why bring him up now that Adam was dead, Adam had never expressed any interest in Terry, the only time I recalled talking about Terry with Adam, Adam had waved it away, he had no interest, it made no difference to him that he had a half brother, and in a way I could understand why he saw it that way, I'm not sure why I sought out Terry at all, I suppose I felt guilty, somehow, for the way my father had dealt with the fact of it, the fact of a son out there in the world that he didn't see, I didn't really know what had happened, maybe my father sent money, maybe he managed to see Terry once in a while without telling anyone in his second family, by second family I mean us, I mean Mom and Adam and Willie and Evan and me, we were the second family, it was hard to think of my father that way, ignoring a son, not supporting his son, I imagined it must have been painful for Terry, although he said no, he hadn't really been concerned about where his father was, and that was because, he said, he, himself, Terry, was on the spectrum, and he looked at things differently because of that, and besides, he said, look how well things had turned out for him, because he had a nice apartment in Chicago, he was a software engineer, he created software having to do with security, protecting data, apparently he made a lot of money, he had a goofy way of talking but apparently he was good at what he did for a living, things had turned out all right for him, it was true, he didn't seem to feel that he had missed anything growing up the way he did, estranged from his father, almost a stranger to his half brothers, in fact from his perspective everything had turned out all right, it was all fine the way he had grown up, but I thought it reflected poorly on my father, I hated to think of my father that way, but I had to think of him that way, he had been distant and quiet, he worked a great deal, he worked for hours over the weekends, he was not the kind of father who played sports with his children, he seemed kind but distant, when we ate dinner he seemed amused by the things we said, we would all talk over one another and he seemed amused, he used to say, I wouldn't mind hearing more about that, it was his catchphrase, I wouldn't mind hearing more about that, and we would all talk over one another some more, and Dad did sometimes tell Adam to let others have a turn, it was hard, honestly, to understand how my father could have turned his back on his first son, Terry, I have a hard time squaring that with my image of him, although it is true he was somewhat distant with us, he was more inclined to be working than spending time with us, he sat for hours out on the porch, papers all over the table out there, working with a pencil, I wonder if he thought he was paying attention to us, working on the porch while we were out in the backyard or running around the park, Short Park, beyond the backyard, or riding bikes on the street out front, he was not paying any attention at all, he was oblivious to the noise we made, he didn't notice when we yelled at each other or cried or even when we were hurt, not that we were often hurt very badly, but it seems odd to remember the way he sat out there, never saying anything to us, never calling out to us, never telling us to be careful, never asking us to keep our voices down, it was as if he had noise-canceling headphones on, that kind of parenting might be seen as negligence these days, certainly I had been more attentive as a father with Muriel, well, I had hovered a little, she was always so tiny and delicate, I called her baby bird, she didn't like it so I stopped, I stopped when she entered kindergarten, I don't like it when you call me baby bird, she told me in her tiny voice, her voice that was like a little bird's voice, I didn't tell her that but that was what her voice was like, maybe if I had had a son rather than a daughter, I would have been less careful, I would have ignored him in the backyard, or on his bicycle, but I couldn't with Em, I couldn't help hovering, worrying, asking if she was all right, bandaging her minor scrapes when they would have been just as well left alone, well, she grew up, she got her ears pierced and then her nose, and then tattoos on her ankles and her wrists, I knew when she got the one tattoo she would get more, that's the way it is with tattoos, you get one and before long you get another, and I turned out to be right, she got four or five of them, who knows when it will stop, she got the first one the same year that Adam died, the moment the tattoo parlors reopened after the Covid lockdowns, she had just turned eighteen, she ran off and got a tattoo with a friend, the friend's parents were livid, I was not livid, the effect was more subtle for me, I felt, somehow, like she wasn't my daughter anymore, the sight of her glittering nose ring and the dark starburst shape on her ankle made her seem strange to me, as if she were someone I didn't know, but that feeling passed, now I was accustomed to the ink under her skin, even the inane words she had needled into her wrist, on the inside of her wrist were the words *never hardly ever*, and when I asked her what it meant she laughed and said it was a joke with a friend, it was their motto, she said, *never hardly ever*, they said it to each other all the time, and so she had gotten a tattoo, well, at the time I wondered how you could permanently mark your skin with a phrase you thought of as a joke, a joke you shared with a high school friend, how could you place a joke on your wrist, forever, a catchphrase, and then I thought of my father, he had his own catchphrase, I wouldn't mind hearing more about that, would he have tattooed that phrase on his wrist, I wondered, of course not, but it was the same as Muriel inking herself, *never hardly ever*, that was no different from I wouldn't mind hearing more about that, really my father's phrase probably would be a better tattoo, wouldn't it, and now Daphne had a tattoo as well, she had gone in with Muriel the second or third time Muriel got a tattoo and got one of her own, Daphne tattooed her wrist, it looked like a slender chain around her wrist, like a bracelet, with four cube-shaped charms, each one with a letter on it, *W-A-I-T*, it said, the letters spelled *WAIT* and I looked at her wrist, the skin was splotchy, and I said, why, what does it mean, *WAIT*, is it a reminder to yourself not to act rashly, no, she said, don't you recognize it, she said, you're the one who taught it to me, Why Am I Talking, she said, W-A-I-T, I learned it from you, it's my mantra now, I learned my mantra from you, you told me it was something you bring up with your clients, and I just loved it, it reminds me to keep calm and not speak until I know the right thing to say, and I was flattered that she would do that, that she would tattoo herself with my catchphrase, or it was her catchphrase but she associated it with me, we had been separated for a long time but we had never gotten divorced, we had gotten past the problem of Jeremy, my old writing partner, who had been her boyfriend originally, but in the end it was me she had put on her wrist, in the end she picked me, she married me, we married and then we separated, we lived separately for a long time, we lived apart but the relationship was never really over, and finally she permanently marked her wrist with words that she associated with me, not with Jeremy, and I wasn't just flattered, I felt victorious, which is silly, I know, but I felt victorious, her tattoo was a sign that I had prevailed over Jeremy, he had had an affair with her while we were married, while he and I were writing partners, in a way he had stolen her back from me, after all, he felt I had stolen her from him, which was insane, considering that he was seeing other women on the side while he was dating her, we were all so young then, but he probably saw it as getting even with me, an affair with my wife was getting even with me, or who knows, maybe they were only thinking of themselves, I have no idea, I was in a free fall at the time, Daphne and I weren't getting along, everything was a mess, who knows what was in Jeremy's or Daphne's mind, they started having sex again, *again*, that's the word I use, but I didn't really know if that was the right word to use, again, maybe they had never stopped, Jeremy was strikingly appealing to women, he had swagger, it was hard to picture him with Daphne, picture him in my mind having sex with Daphne, but I was accustomed to the fact of it now, I had accustomed myself to the idea that my wife had been unfaithful to me, it had been difficult, it was, now that I think of it, not so dissimilar to Muriel's tattoos, to the way that Em seemed like a stranger to me when she got her piercings and her tattoos, similarly Daphne seemed like a stranger to me when I learned she had been fucking Jeremy again, if again is the right word, maybe they had never really stopped, but in any case I became accustomed to it, it became a part of her, it was a marring of her surface, like a tattoo, but I could make myself see beyond it, or I suppose I just reached a point that I did not feel the need to look at it and think about it every time I saw her, and then she got her tattoo, her *W-A-I-T* tattoo, it was a mind trick I sometimes raised with my clients at work, I had taught it to Daphne, Why Am I Talking, it was just a reminder to listen for a moment, in any case I had taught Daphne that phrase and she had tattooed it on her wrist

And where was Daphne, I wondered, looking up from my notes, she had wanted to say a few words, that's the phrase they use for these things, memorial services, say a few words, she didn't think my mother would speak, she was probably right, my mother wouldn't likely speak in Adam's memory, even now, two years after he had died, there was bad blood between them, well, there had never been good blood, if that's a thing, good blood, sometimes I think the only good blood in the family was with Evan, the baby, he was so much younger than the rest of us, my mother somehow seemed like a different woman around Evan, she laughed at his jokes, she called him several times a week, and he called her several times a week, they spoke on the phone almost every day, what they talked about I don't know, Evan seemed irritated when I asked him about that once, I asked, how do you have anything to talk about with her every day, what do you say to each other, and he said, I tell her about my day, what do you think we talk about, we talk about our day, what we did that day, or the day before, and I could hear real anger in his voice, I was surprised how irritated he seemed by my question, so I said, I just wondered, that's all, but in my mind I couldn't imagine exactly what they had to report on, day after day, did they talk about their meals, for instance, did she tell him what she had cooked for Carl's breakfast, did he tell her what he had observed on his commute, I could not quite see how they had anything new to report to each other on a day-to-day basis, of course married couples do that, they speak every day, the healthy couples speak every day, but that's a couple, somehow it seems different with a mother and her grown son, maybe that was why Evan was so irritated by my asking what he talked about with Mom, maybe he sensed that there was something immature, let's face it, infantile, about it, but on the other hand I was jealous, I didn't understand his relationship with my mother, I guess somehow she had mellowed by the time she had him, or she had found a way to block out the fighting between Adam and Willie and me, by then she knew how to retreat to the kitchen or the little yellow room, she would bring Evan with her in his rocker seat, when he got bigger he had a scooting table, Evan sat in that in the kitchen and scooted around on the linoleum, there was a gate on the doorway so he couldn't push out into the rest of the house, and my mother would block him from the little yellow room, just set her legs in the doorway so he couldn't get by, the two of them were cordoned off back there in the kitchen area, I don't know, somehow Mom got along with Evan in a way she had never gotten along with the rest of us, it's not unusual, love doesn't get doled out evenly in families, for some reason Evan brought out Mom's softer side, even now that she was more than eighty years old and he was forty, she looked at him the way I remembered looking at Muriel when she was an infant, somehow Mom had finally found a child to dote on, maybe it was just because he was the last, she was pretty old when he was born, it was unusual to have a baby at that age back then, he hadn't been planned, he was an unexpected addition to the family, thinking back on the way the three of us, Adam and Willie and I, had fought and scratched and shouted, who would have thought my mother would have doted on Evan the way she did, she didn't push him out into the fray with the older boys, she kept him safe behind the gate in the kitchen area, and when he was just thirteen or fourteen, the three of us older boys were already mostly gone, Adam barely ever came home from school, he found a place to live in the city each summer, rather than live and work in Amory, with all the rest of us around, and meanwhile Willie, well, Willie had died, Willie was gone, and then I went to college, and I was like Adam, I mostly didn't come home once I was in college, I stuck around on campus during summer breaks and I worked as a security guard or in the library, there were jobs on campus and I could stay there and never go home, that was how Adam handled it too, and I suppose that was one way that Adam and I were similar, when we left for college we didn't come home much anymore, we stayed away from Amory, he began setting up a path for himself in New York, he knew what he wanted, he wanted money, he wanted to be rich, he had said as much to my parents, to all of us, we were arguing about something when he was only fifteen or sixteen, and he said, this is why I'm going to be rich, so I don't worry about this picayune bullshit, yes, he said picayune bullshit, I actually laughed at him for using such an odd phrase, I think we had been arguing about new sneakers, I don't know why, someone needed new sneakers and my mother wanted to hold off and my father said, oh go ahead and get them, and my mother was irritated, she told him he never paid enough attention to expenses, she said, you call yourself an accountant but you don't even know what a pair of shoes costs, at that point she was working part-time at her sister's shop, Aunt Ellen had a crafts shop, my mother handled the register most afternoons, once Evan was in school, I doubt she made much money, it was probably nothing, but the two of them, Ellen and my mother, were close, if Mom hadn't been working for Ellen at the craft shop she would have been talking with Ellen on the phone, so it made sense to just go down to the shop and sit behind the counter, and Evan would walk to the shop after school and do his homework there, it was another refuge for the two of them, the older boys weren't welcome at the shop, it sold yarn and needlepoint kits and that kind of thing, I remember my mother telling one of us, probably Adam, that he couldn't come into the shop, he would just start roughhousing in there, he would be too wild, it was probably true but it seems cruel, thinking back on it, to have told him that, and then Willie, Willie loved sewing and crafting, but she didn't like him to come in, it's not for boys, she said, she was uncomfortable with Willie's interest in sewing, it wasn't until he was in high school that he could really do any sewing, he signed up to work in the theater, sewing costumes, no one ever said, that's funny, your mother works in a sewing shop and now you're sewing at school, no, he didn't spend any time at the shop, my mother didn't bring him kits from the shop, she could have but she wasn't comfortable with his interest in sewing, she knew she could have been better with Willie, she used to say, who knew anything about gay people back then, she said, I didn't want to admit he was gay, AIDS was everywhere, I was just hiding him from it, I thought I was hiding him from it, well, that was a tragedy, he spent his last days at home in bed, emaciated, you could see the bones in his arms and his face, he was wasting away, he barely had the strength to drink from his milkshake, Mom had never been able to face the reality that Willie was gay, maybe if she had let him into the craft shop, maybe if she had encouraged him to sew, well, no, what good would that have done, and it occurred to me that she hadn't helped Willie when he was in need, she hadn't helped Dad, and she didn't help Adam when he needed help either, but maybe it wouldn't have done Adam any good anyway, her help wouldn't have made any difference to Willie in the end, and probably the same goes for Adam

It was getting late, I thought, looking around the meeting room at the Amory Public Library, there were maybe ten people there now, but no Daphne and Muriel, no Mom and Carl, no Evan, he said he would come but he wasn't going to bring his wife, who was pregnant, why should she come, he asked me over the phone, what's the point, I don't even know why I'm coming, or that's not true, I'm coming for you, Randy, I'm doing it for you, but Rachel is almost eight months pregnant so I'm not going to make her drive four hours for a memorial service for someone she's never met, and someone who, by the way, bullied me through my childhood, not just me, he bullied you too, so I'm coming to show my support for you, that's the only reason I'm coming, but even so Evan wasn't there yet, he hadn't arrived, Daphne and Muriel hadn't arrived, and my mother and Carl were not there, there were just people from Amory, I recognized some of them but not all of them, I wondered what they knew about our family, I wondered how our family had appeared to the people we knew in town, we probably seemed like a normal family, a big family, a noisy family, a successful family, all the children went to college, that was a marker in Amory, it was still a blue-collar town back then, not everyone went to college, not everyone could afford it, not that we could afford it, money was tight, of course it was tight, there were four children, my father wasn't a wealthy man, think of that fight over sneakers, think of Adam saying he was going to get rich, he wasn't going to worry about picayune bullshit, in the end he was poor, he was nearly broke, he had come to me looking for a loan, but I hadn't understood, I thought he was trying to get me to invest in something, all he wanted was a loan, I didn't see what was obvious, he was broke and he needed money, he had no way of making money, he had been banned from the financial industry, he had been entangled in lawsuits with his former employer, not to mention legal battles over real estate, he needed money desperately, I didn't understand that, if only he had come to me maybe I could have helped, not that I had that much money, still, I might have been able to help, but he didn't ask outright, he didn't ask me for a loan that day in Grand Central, at the bar in Grand Central, he acted like I was an idiot, an idiot about money, like I needed his guidance, instead of just saying *he* needed money, if he had asked me I would have found a way to help, I had some money here and there, I had retirement funds, but being honest with myself, I don't know, maybe I wouldn't have sent him money, or I don't know if I had enough to help him, I had a daughter and we were saving for college, I was lucky, we were lucky, Daphne and I were lucky, we couldn't have afforded it without the money from *Catbirds*, still, it's not as if we were rolling in dough, as they say, we had a lot of expenses, so maybe I wouldn't have given Adam money, or maybe I wouldn't have had enough to really help him, he probably needed much more than I could provide, I don't know, of course I feel ashamed of myself for not realizing that he was asking me for money, he needed money, he wasn't running some kind of stock fund, he just wanted money, but he had been so abrasive I walked away, I just left him there in Cipriani with his vodka tonic and dish of olives, I couldn't stand to be with him one second more, so who knows, maybe I wouldn't have lent him money, or given

him money, that's really what he needed, he hadn't worked in
years, he was out of cash, he was out of luck, and I didn't know
it until after he died but he went to my mother, it was hard
to imagine, Adam approaching Mom for money, she told me
about it after he died, she told me that he had called her asking
for money for health insurance and other expenses, and she
said no, she said no

Toward the end of his life, Adam was struggling with some serious health problems, it was all related to diabetes, well, not the mental health problems, but he had neuropathy of the feet, the stinging needles in his feet, he was probably going to need to have a foot amputated, I didn't know this, he hadn't told me about it, if I had known, if my mother had known, I don't think she knew about it, I didn't know about it, also his eyesight was failing, and he had gained even more weight, I didn't know any of this, the last time I spoke to him was at the beginning of the pandemic, I didn't want to speak to him, but I thought of him alone in lockdown, I wasn't alone, not like that, I was spending more time with Daphne, our old dog was sick, Gnarls Barkley we called him, that was a popular band when we got him as a puppy, we thought it would be funny to call him Gnarls Barkley after the band, but Daphne always called him Gnarly, anyway, Gnarly was sick, Daphne was stressing out about the dog, it was the beginning of the pandemic, she felt anxious, she needed help, so I came over to spend time with her and Gnarly and Muriel, we called ourselves a pod, but it wasn't a pod, it was our family resuming, reforming, but Adam was alone, *toward the end of his life he was suffering from diabetes, among other things his eyesight was failing, and he may have gotten lost or discombobulated and fallen into a canal in Ogden, where he was living at the time of his death, we don't really know, no one really knows*, I had called him at the beginning of the pandemic, when everyone was supposed to stay inside, I called him to check on him, to ask how he was doing, just to say hello, and when I called him he picked up and didn't say anything, he picked up and I could hear him breathing, Adam, I said, Adam, are you there, can you hear me, Adam, I said, it's Randy, and he asked me where I was calling from, was I calling from a secure location, and I laughed, that's how stupid I was, I laughed when he asked if I was calling from a secure location, I said, you've been watching too many spy movies, but anyway, I was just calling to see how you were doing, and he said, I'm sick, and that brought me up short, it was just at the beginning of the pandemic, no one really understood what Covid was, although already there was talk that it was bad for people who were overweight, and Adam was heavy, he was very heavy at that point, in fact he was even heavier than I had known, he had gained a considerable amount of weight since the last time I had seen him, but I didn't know that at the time, just that he was heavy, and that could be dangerous with Covid, I knew that much, what's wrong, I asked him, and he told me he had chills and he had been throwing up, but he was feeling better, he told me, he was feeling better and he thought he might go to the supermarket for a few things, now that he had finished throwing up, oh no, I said, don't do that, don't go out, can you order some food, can you have something delivered, you shouldn't go to a store if you've been throwing up, I tried to persuade him not to go out, I don't know what he did in the end, I remember thinking, well, maybe he's not really sick if he can go to the supermarket, and I fretted over it, I wasn't sure what to do, he lived alone, was he sick, did he have Covid, I wondered if I could find someone to go to his apartment, knock on his door, but I had never been to that apartment, I hadn't visited him in several years, the last time I had seen him was in

Cipriani, in Grand Central, when he made the comment about Muriel, it's hard to believe a brother would say such a thing, but that was Adam, sadly that was Adam, and it doesn't reflect well on me but I didn't follow up after that first call at the beginning of the lockdown, as we called it then, although we weren't actually locked down, we could go out, anyway, I kept thinking of the last time I had seen Adam, that time in Grand Central, it wasn't just that he complained about his drink, it wasn't just that he made the comment about Muriel and the fact that she didn't look like me, but there was also something he said about Willie, he said Willie had gone to some crap art school in North Carolina, Willie, who had died before he could complete even three semesters of college, and all he wanted was to stay there in North Carolina, I imagined he finally felt at home there, I imagined a campus full of boys like Willie, gay boys finally released from their homes and flowering there in North Carolina, under the southern sun, and when Adam referred to it as some crap art school in North Carolina, that was the phrase he used, who had ever heard of that place, he asked, when he said that I thought I might just punch him right there in the restaurant, I felt such rage at him that I actually had to sit on my hands, I told myself to stay calm, not to respond, and as my breathing slowed I realized I would never have to see him again, I would never do this again, because Adam hadn't actually cared about seeing me or hearing about me, all he wanted was for me to invest in some scheme, or that's what I thought then, I only came to realize later he was looking for a loan, he needed money, he was broke, but whatever it was that he had come for, his motive was different from mine, I was trying to stay in touch with my brother, because our family was dwindling, Willie was dead, my father was dead, and Mom was remarried and it was a little as if she had inserted herself in a new family, she lived in her new husband's house, she was close with his daughters, they all spent time together at Carl's house in Vermont, summers and winters, she was too old for skiing or hiking, but Carl's daughters, and his daughters' families, spent weeks and weeks there, and Mom seemed to have adopted them, or more like they had adopted her, it was like getting a pain-free bonus family for her, she stepped out of her old life and all the complications of her sons, living and dead, and stepped into a new, simple role, she was Momma Cary in her new family, the grandchildren called her that, they seemed to love her, she took up cooking, which she had never liked doing when she was raising her own family, I can understand that, feeding four sons, putting food out day after day, I get it, it probably wasn't much fun, she didn't have any interest in food at that point, it was just one meal after another, morning after morning, night after night, we didn't eat very well, Mom wasn't worried about healthy food, we all ate cold cereal each morning, even Dad, he liked cereal as much as the rest of us, we went through massive amounts of cereal, all the sweet stuff, Fruity Pebbles, Life, Frosted Mini-Wheats, she wouldn't buy the chocolate cereals, I suppose that was where she drew the line on healthy eating, no chocolate cereal for breakfast, no Cookie Crisp cereal, hard to believe they could market a food that was basically miniature chocolate chip cookies as a breakfast cereal, but they did, anyway, she got older, she finally quit smoking, that was the only demand Carl made of her, he got her to quit smoking when nobody else could do it, not that she was particularly healthy, she was in her eighties and she had smoked a lot of cigarettes in her life, she had an alarming cough, anyway, she had just walked into this new family, Carl's family, she had walked in and never really looked back, she still spoke with Evan almost every day, plus

Evan was great friends with Carl, Evan had a relationship with the whole family, but I didn't, I was off in California, so it felt in a way like there was almost no one left in my own family, Dad gone, Willie gone, Mom sealed up in her new family, Evan in Philadelphia, Adam in Connecticut, and meanwhile I had only one child, little Muriel, Em, we called her, Little Moohoo, that was all that was left of our family, when things closed down for Covid, I called Mom, then I called Evan, and finally I decided to call Adam, but that was a challenge for me, it took a while to persuade myself to call up his number on my phone, I still remembered our cocktail in Grand Central, I hadn't expected to speak with him again, but I did it, after all we were still family, I called him, and after I hung up I worried that I should call again, just to find out if he was really sick, he seemed somewhat out of it, that is, it was odd that he would say he was going to go to the supermarket so soon after being sick, and yet I didn't call him back, I never did follow up, after a week or two I forgot about it, I forgot about him, I guess you could say, although I didn't really forget about him, but each day that went by I figured, well, if he were actually sick he would have let me know, although I knew he probably wouldn't, but I told myself that, and I thought about him a little less each day, I was busy, I was trying to figure out how to see clients over video, I was busy, really busy, old clients showed up in my inbox out of the blue, people I hadn't seen in a year or two, mostly teenage clients who suddenly had to move back in with their parents, they were under a lot of stress, I was seeing more than twenty-five clients a week, it was more than I could handle, but in any case Adam just drifted out of my mind, I stopped thinking about him, which incidentally was preferable to me, I didn't *want* to think about Adam, I was happy not to think about him, I had reached out to him at the beginning of the lockdown, as they called it, that was enough, I had done my part, and then I let him slip out of mind, and I didn't think of him for a couple months, when my mother called to tell me the police had contacted her and said that Adam was dead, he had been found floating in a canal off the Housatonic River, and she wanted me to go there to deal with it, so I went to Ogden and persuaded Evan to drive up from Philadelphia and help me clear out his apartment, and we did it, we dealt with his apartment, his car, his belongings, but we didn't arrange for a funeral or a memorial service, all we did was have his body cremated

It wasn't until Adam died and I was staying in his apartment that I really thought about the strange thing he said when I called him that last time, he asked if I was calling from a secure location, and I wondered what he had meant by that, and then there was the gun in his bureau, I didn't understand why it was there, it made no sense, was he afraid, was the neighborhood dangerous, it was run-down but it seemed safe enough to me, the apartment building had a parking lot outside with no fence or locks or anything like that, there was no one hanging around on the street, although it was still early after the lockdown when I was there, maybe it would have been different under normal circumstances, anyway, there was the gun and the fact that he was floating in a canal with no wallet, and there were the prescriptions I had found, the drugs weren't written out to him, and I wondered about that, I called my mother, why she would have known, I don't know, but I called her and she was irritated, irritated with me for asking about Adam, she didn't know anything about it, she hadn't heard from him in weeks or months, she couldn't remember, she said, he had wanted her to put him on her insurance, how could she do that, she said to me, how could she put him on her Medicare, of course she couldn't do that, and her supplemental insurance was only for herself, it didn't cover children who were adults, she said, he should be looking into Obamacare, she said she told him, she couldn't do anything about him being on her insurance, it was ridiculous, and as for her paying for his insurance, well, she told him she didn't have money for that, she didn't have much money, her husband was the one with the money, not that he had much money, she told me, but he had more money than she did, and, she told me, that's what she told Adam, but Adam wouldn't listen, he had asked before and she said, I can't understand it, she told me she said, I can't understand why you can't use Obamacare, isn't that the whole point of it, but he seemed to think there were problems with Obamacare, my mother told me, Adam wasn't able to make the website work, it was something like that, she said to me, those were her words, it was something like that, and I said, well, I wish he had come to me, I didn't understand, and it was true, I hadn't understood, if I had known that he didn't even have insurance, health insurance, I might have helped him, but my mother dismissed that idea, what could you have done, she asked me, you have a daughter to take care of, she's starting college soon, you couldn't have been expected to take care of Adam as well, and I said, listen, Mom, I don't understand why you're getting so angry, if I had known—but she cut me off and she said, I'm angry because he threatened me, yes, that's right, he threatened me, she said, he said, I'll make you pay, and she repeated what he had said to her, I'll make you pay, did he really say that, I asked her, he said that, she told me, he said, I'll make you pay, and while we were having this conversation, I was sitting in Adam's dim living room, what had been Adam's dim living room, it was a hot day, it was hot for early June, I had cleared out most of the apartment, there wasn't much left, we had got rid of almost everything, it was sad how little Adam had owned that was worth saving, some photo albums, a good watch, I remembered that Adam had boasted long ago about having several watches that were worth more than fifty thousand dollars, now there seemed to be only one left, it wasn't worth much as it turned out, well, it was worth maybe five thousand, based on some web searches, there were no fifty-thousand-dollar watches that we could find, that one last watch seemed to be the only valuable thing left in Adam's entire life, and before I hung up, I asked Mom to clarify what Adam had said, when he said, I'll make you pay, did he mean he was going to make her pay for the insurance somehow, or was it more of a threat, like a mobster would say, I'll make you pay, but my mother brushed it away, who knows, she said to me, I just hung up on him, he was unhinged and I hung up on him, and I said, and was that the last time you spoke with him, that was it, she said, that was the last time Adam and I spoke, he told me he would make me pay and I slammed the phone down and we never spoke again, it's sad but I didn't like the tone he was taking and I had already told him I couldn't pay for his insurance and so that was the last time we spoke

*Adam wasn't well toward the end of his life, he had diabetes, he was
having some trouble getting around because he had gained weight
and his eyesight was iffy, particularly at night, and unfortunately
he had some issues with doctors and with insurance, and he resorted
to self-medication*, is that the right phrase, self-medication, well,
in any case, I shouldn't even bring that up, Adam's old football
buddies, the few other people gathering here in the meeting
room at the Amory Public Library, none of them would want
to hear about Adam's medications, this was not the place,
probably I was the only person here who cared about Adam's
medications, well, Julia Slotkin also cared, Julia Slotkin, that
was the name on the plastic medical bottles, most of them,
most of the prescriptions had been made out to her, and
actually it turned out that when Adam had died, she had come
to the apartment to get them back, I learned that later, when
I was cleaning out his place, he had been dead for a month by
then, it took a while to identify him, since he didn't have any
ID on him when he died, where was the wallet, that still ate
at me, why didn't the police wonder about it, but they were
busy with everything else that was going on, Covid-19, Black
Lives Matter, whatever, I was carrying a bag of garbage out of
Adam's apartment, a bag full of worthless papers, when Adam's
neighbor, an old woman who lived in the next apartment,
stopped me in the hall and asked if I had found the girl, she said,
did you find the girl, but it was hard to hear her, because she

was wearing a mask and hugging a grocery bag to her chest, she was trying to manage the bag and to get her keys from her purse, and she was old, and the mask probably wasn't helping with her breathing, so I had to ask her to repeat herself, and she needed a moment to get enough breath to ask me, did I find the girl, I shook my head, I wasn't looking for a girl, I was just trying to clean out Adam's apartment, at first I thought maybe the old woman was confused, it was a confusing time, Covid-19, Black Lives Matter, even in that run-down little town of Ogden, even in Ogden there were marches and the police had used tear gas, if I were an old woman living in the Treadway apartment building, I might have been confused and frightened, it was strange enough as it was being *me*, it was confusing and frightening to be entombed in Adam's dark and dingy apartment, which he hadn't paid rent on since October, he was six months behind on his rent, although he hadn't seen it that way, I had read through his folders, the papers marked up with *FU*, *FU*, *FU*, I could hear him hollering at me, *fuck you fuck you fuck you*, but it was just notes to follow up, disputes with the building management company, supposedly the elevator was out of service for two days in September, and that rendered the apartment unusable, that was Adam's argument, and he wanted a discount for his trouble, and then there were heating issues, and noise issues, and a problem with the kitchen drain, all of these disputes at once, one after another, Adam was like one of those plate-spinning acts, how did he keep them all spinning all at once, how could he add any more, Adam just kept it all going, and it wasn't just the apartment, it was the utilities, his car lease, a dentist, a dentist he hadn't seen in three years, Adam was still locked in a fight with the dentist and some kind of collection company, I should have understood right away that Adam was broke, but it didn't occur to me, even when I

looked at his bank account and brokerage account, there wasn't
much there, but I just assumed there was some other account,
he had wanted to set up some kind of offshore account for me,
so I figured he must have done the same for himself, I figured
he had a huge stash somewhere, Switzerland or the Cayman
Islands or wherever it is that people hide money, I assumed that
was what Adam had done, and the disputes with his landlord
and everyone else, the dentist, everyone, it was just Adam's
nature, his combativeness, his *bellicosity*, knowing how much
money he had made as a young man, that incredible house in
Greenwich with the built-in music system, five bedrooms, also
he had had a Porsche and a BMW, all of this by the time he
was thirty, thirty-one, although of course that had been a long
time back, it was about twenty years ago, but I just didn't think
of Adam as broke or poor, even when his poverty was staring
me in the face, even when I looked through Adam's folders,
the papers detailing his spiraling disputes with, it seemed,
practically everyone in the state of Connecticut, I didn't think
Adam was broke, I just thought he was being himself, he loved
a fight, that was his pleasure in life, that was what I thought,
it was stupid of me, I was *blind*, I was blind to the reality, it
was staring me in the face, and the same thing was true about
Julia Slotkin, when the old woman down the hall asked me if
I had found the girl, I had no idea what she was talking about,
I couldn't see what should have been obvious to me

I don't know why it took me so long to wonder about the name Julia Slotkin, I guess I was in a kind of fog, there was so much going on, Adam's death and everything else, but I did finally put it together, the name on the prescription medications, the name on the card, the card that was in the drawer with the gun, anyway, I finally got her phone number and address online, she was a lawyer, or, she referred to herself as an attorney, I said, Julia, are you a lawyer, she corrected me, she said, I'm an attorney, as if I had misspoken by calling her a lawyer, that was her manner, that was her way of speaking, and she was distrustful, at least she was distrustful of me, she didn't want to meet at first, in fact she said she had nothing to say to me, I have nothing to say to any of you, she told me the first time I called her, I wasn't sure what she was talking about, any of you, she said, what did that mean, I have nothing to say to any of you, she was combative, that was the word, I thought, oh, this reminds me of Adam, that's what I thought, but also she was suspicious, she almost didn't say anything at first, I called up, I was wearing earphones, earbuds, I told her who I was, I was Adam Green's younger brother, and she didn't say anything for a long time, but I knew she was there, I could hear her breathing, it was like she was inside me, in my head, breathing quietly, she sounded frightened, her breath was ragged, and finally I said, I don't know if you know, I'm sorry to tell you this, but Adam died a few weeks ago, and her breath caught a little, I think her breath caught a little, but she still didn't say anything, she just breathed, breathed in and out in my head, it was strange, it was like there was no barrier between us, it was like we were somehow one creature, I felt freaked out by her breathing and her silence and I said, Julia, are you there, are you all right, and she said, I have nothing to say to any of you, that was when she said, I have nothing to say to any of you, and then she hung up on me

I was hoping Julia wouldn't turn up for the memorial service,
I admit it, but now there were ten or twelve people in the
audience, people from Amory, people who had known Adam as
a child, people who had known our family back in the 1980s, I
saw a woman who had lived down the block from us, I nodded
to her and she made a namaste to me, we didn't speak, she was
talking to one of Adam's football buddies, but it was more
than I had expected, it wasn't like the crowd, hundreds of
people, who had come to Willie's service in the auditorium,
that was different, but even a dozen people was more than I
had expected, I had half expected it would only be us, Mom and
Carl, me and Daphne and Muriel, and Evan, that was it, and
I had been afraid that Julia would show up and it would just
be us, just the family members and Julia Slotkin, she had told
me she wanted to speak at the service, she had some things she
wanted to say, she told me she was the one who actually cared
about him and therefore it was only fair for her to speak at his
memorial service, it wasn't the kind of thing you want to hear,
planning for a memorial service, an angry woman wanting to
get things off her chest, you abandoned him, she told me, and
then she said, I didn't abandon him, I deserve to speak, so I
said, well, I said, I guess, I guess, yes, if you feel strongly about
it, you can speak at the service, it will probably only be a small
group, mostly family members, but you are welcome to speak,

and the more I thought about it, I thought, why not, why not
let her speak her mind, she had ideas about Adam, ideas about
Adam and the family, she could air her thoughts, she could
make some pointed comments, but once I told her she was
welcome to come to the service and to speak, she faltered a
little, she said, I don't know how I'm going to get there, I don't
own a car, she said, and I thought, well, Amory wasn't that far
from Milford, where she lived, Milford was basically on the
opposite side of New Haven from Amory, it was probably half
an hour door-to-door and if Julia couldn't figure out how to
make the trip that would be fine, I thought, and we didn't speak
again after that, so I didn't know, as I stood in the back aisle of
the meeting room at the Amory Public Library, whether Julia
would actually show up, or read the statement she had written,
she emailed me the statement she planned to read, that was
her word for it, a statement, not a eulogy or a remembrance,
a statement, and it was about what I had expected, *Hello, I am
Julia Slotkin, I'm an attorney living in Milford. I met Adam several
years ago, not long after he moved to Ogden, when he needed legal
representation, and we became friends after that, in truth we were
closer than friends, we were more than friends. We shared certain
experiences in life and that made us close. Most importantly, we were
alienated from our families, more than that, we were excluded from
them, and we gave each other the kind of support that we might have
expected or hoped to have received from parents, brothers, sisters,
and loved ones. We had to provide that to each other. No one seems
to know what Adam was doing on the night he died, or no one wants
to admit it, but I do know that Adam had grown unstable in the
months before he died and it fell to me to provide support. There
were other people that could have stepped up but they did not, so I
did, and I don't regret it. I may be the only one in the world who*

will miss Adam, who misses him even now, but I know that I was his support system, his helper, his sounding board, his adviser, and he was mine. I will miss him and I simply wanted to say that: I will miss him. Will you?

Well, of course I would prefer that Julia not read that statement, I didn't much want to force everyone to hear that, but on the other hand it was true that she missed Adam in a way that no one else did, it was sad but it was true, she was right, she was the only one who missed him, although she was overstating things, I thought, she hadn't known Adam all that long, and it was hard to say just how close they had been, I mean, I didn't get the sense that they were lovers, they didn't have sex, as far as I could tell, I asked her about that, I didn't say, Julia, did you sleep with Adam, but I asked about the nature of their relationship, were they a couple, I asked, I wasn't sure, I told her, that's why I was asking, and she said, God, everything Adam said about you is true, that was how she responded when I asked, essentially innocently, if they were a couple, if they were boyfriend and girlfriend, this happened, I think, the second time I called her up, after she had hung up on me, I waited a day and I called her up again, I had so many questions for her, I was just trying to fill in the blanks about Adam's life, the later part of his life, oh, that's rich, she said, you wanted to hear about the last months of his life but you don't know anything about him, you don't know anything about his life, his life wasn't just the last few months, it was a whole life, and I said, whoa, I said, Julia, please, whoa, I don't really know you, I only learned about you from seeing your name among Adam's things, that's why I'm calling, and she said, well, I know about you, I know all about you, you're the writer, you wrote that movie, you're Mr. Hollywood, and I thought it was strange that she would call me that, Mr. Hollywood, and then she said, yes, you see, she said, I even know your code name, and she went on like that for a while, me being a screenwriter, I was famous, I had run off to California, and I had to interrupt her, I had to explain that Adam had misled her, or no, he had misspoken, I wasn't a screenwriter, I had been a screenwriter, but I was a therapist now, I worked with teenagers and their families, I didn't have anything to do with the movie business, Adam always overstated my success, I had written a story, "Catbirds," and it was turned into a movie, maybe she had seen it, but the movie wasn't anything like the story, it had been revised so often that the movie almost had nothing to do with the original story, originally it had been a story about Willie, Willie's death, and the impact it had on our family, well, it was fictionalized, but that was the basis, and by the time it became a movie, the character that was Willie, the Willie figure, was not even gay, he did not die from AIDS, it was a different story, it was fine, it was a fine screenplay, it was a good movie, but it didn't have much to do with what actually happened in my family, it just seemed that way because I had written it, because I had a brother who had died, and people were confused about that, and I explained all that to Julia, I explained that Adam often seemed not to understand that I wasn't a famous screenwriter, I had never been a famous screenwriter, I was a therapist, that's all, and after explaining all that, Julia's first response was to say, well, I'm not surprised to hear how you immediately rush to impugn Adam's memory and the way he spoke of you, and that was the way she spoke, she used words like *impugn* and *attorney*, she used them like sharp little sticks, like needles that she poked at me, and there was a part of me that thought, well, forget it, why bother with this woman, she seems deranged, but I was speaking to her from Adam's apartment, his dingy little apartment in the Treadway building, with the flickering bulbs in the hallways and the tortoise-slow elevators, and I remembered the canal where João had pointed to where he had found Adam, floating face down in the water, and I felt sad for Adam, I felt sad for Julia, I didn't even know her, but I felt sad for her, her anger and her temper reminded me of Adam, not in a good way or a bad way, really, it just seemed that Adam's belligerent spirit had carried forward into Julia, not that I believed in anything like that, in souls or spirits, but it was odd, hearing Julia speak, I recognized the angry cadences of her voice, you could hear Adam in there, it was like he was trapped in there, imprisoned in her rib cage, banging to get out

My mother finally arrived at five minutes to eleven, she and Carl arrived together, she approached me, I approached her, we approached each other and she made *mwah* sounds, that's the way she greets her children, she shies away from human contact, I only noticed this as an adult, I don't think it occurred to me when I was younger, she and Carl don't touch very often, sometimes I've seen him grab her hand when they're walking, she allows that, but she's not a hugger, not a kisser, not really a *toucher*, I remember her putting a cool compress on my forehead when I had a fever as a child, it was Lyme disease, it nearly sent me to the hospital, she sat on the edge of my bed and held a damp washcloth on my forehead, anyway, here in the library, finally, she shuffled over to me, she's not very steady on her feet, *mwah mwah*, she said, and I shook Carl's hand, he still had a firm grip, he called me Evan and then Adam and finally hit on my name, Randy, he said, he was frustrated with himself, he grimaced, misnaming me, he knew my name, his mind was playing tricks on him, my mother didn't care, she didn't even seem to notice Carl was having trouble speaking, she said they had been sitting out in the car in the parking lot, we just sat there for twenty minutes, she said, isn't that awful, I couldn't bear to come in early, I couldn't bear people coming up to me, I'm just awful, oh, you're not so bad, Carl said, oh, no, she said, I'm awful, and she told me, just take me to my seat, I don't want to speak to anyone, I just want to sit down,

I'll sit with Carl, we'll sit with Evan and Daphne and Muriel and we'll get this over with, I know it's awful of me, I just wish this was all over with, who are all these people, I don't recognize a soul, who is that woman waving to us, is that Lisa, God, I can't think of her children's names, I guess we have to say hello, and she went off to see her old neighbor, she even seemed to have a bit of energy in her step, she hadn't expected any of her old acquaintances to be there, we had all left Amory years ago, after Willie died and I started college, the marriage only lasted a couple more years, and Dad was sick and moved to an apartment in New Haven, Mom remarried, that wasn't Carl, her second marriage didn't last long but it took her out of Amory, she moved farther north in Connecticut, up to the Hartford area, somehow she found boyfriends very quickly, she was never single for long, that second marriage happened so quickly that some people assumed she had been having an affair, but she probably hadn't, I don't think she did, of course I don't like to think that she could have been sleeping around behind Dad's back, but I actually don't think she did, it wasn't her style, she just plunged into relationships, it seemed to me, she met Dad and married him within three months, that marriage lasted more than twenty years, and then she met her second husband, his name was Arthur, Art, he used to call himself Artie, Artie my boy, he would say to himself, Art died maybe a year into their marriage, he died before Dad did, in fact, and I remember taking some satisfaction from that, my mother's new husband had died before her old one did, Dad was sick, he was weak, living alone in New Haven, I had a hard time forgiving Mom for abandoning the marriage, although she claims it wasn't that way, they agreed to split up, Mom and Dad agreed to a separation and a divorce, once Evan was off to college, they lasted that long, that was the idea, hang on until Evan was off to college, but by then Dad was getting weak, he needed medical assistance, it just didn't sit right with me, I had a hard time forgiving her for that, I knew that losing Willie was a blow, I suppose that's all it was, Willie's death blew the marriage apart, she needed a fresh start, she found Artie, he was older, Artie my boy, he seemed like a nice guy, it was sad that he died so suddenly, but then she found Carl, barely six months later she was seeing Carl, he was a widower, he had children of his own, they spent a lot of time together, Carl's family and Mom, they melded into a new family, I suppose, it wasn't as complicated as ours, no one had died of AIDS, there was no one like Adam lingering angrily in the background, no father withering away with Huntington's, plus Carl was loaded, he seemed rich, he had a grand house in Vermont, when he retired they moved there full-time, a big house up near Montpelier, a lot of land, a mudroom full of skis and snowshoes and tennis rackets, Carl loved activities like that, hitting a tennis ball, skeet shooting, he owned several shotguns and taught my mother how to shoot, it was odd to think of her with a shotgun in her hand, but she really knew how to use it, I hadn't spent much time at Carl's house in Vermont, but after Adam died I drove up to the house with a few boxes of belongings, that was all that was worth keeping, just three or four boxes, and I had the pistol in one of the boxes, it was wrapped up in an old sweater that I had duct-taped into a kind of lump, I didn't know how to store it or carry it, I didn't know what to do with it, so I wrapped it up as best as I could and I drove to Vermont, and while I was visiting, I asked Carl what I should do with the gun, he had shotguns, he knew a bit about guns, we unwrapped it together in the kitchen, whew, Carl said, this thing is loaded, you've been driving around with a loaded pistol, so I had been right, Carl knew about guns, he removed the bullets, it was a cartridge, and Carl looked it over and said it was in working order, and he called out to Mom in the other room, Cary, come take a look at this, Adam really did have a gun, Randy brought it up from Connecticut, he said, and Mom shuffled into the kitchen, she has a kind of unsteady gait now, she doesn't walk really upright, she drags her feet a little, or she doesn't quite lift them up all the way when she walks, it's a *shiff-shiff-shiff* sound, anyway, she came into the kitchen and took a look at the gun on the kitchen table, it's in good working order, Carl said, what do you think about that, and my mother leaned over the gun for a minute, so, she said, he really did have a gun, she said, he told me he had one and it turns out he actually did have one, she said, he told me he would kill me, he said he would shoot me, and when Mom told me that, I wasn't sure what to think, I couldn't really imagine Adam making threats like that, he was more of a lawsuit person, but there was the gun on the kitchen table, there were the bullets, and I didn't know my mother to be a liar or even, really, someone who exaggerated about things, honestly I could think of nothing to say to that, to the idea that Adam would have threatened to shoot Mom, they had never liked one another, as far as I know, they had always clashed, somehow, it's hard to understand how a mother cannot like her son, well, to be completely honest, it wasn't just that she didn't like him, it was more that she didn't love him, I don't understand it, I'll never understand that, but she didn't love Adam, I don't think, she would sometimes say things like, well, of course I love Adam but I can't stand the way he acts with his football friends, or she would say to him, I love you but you must keep out of the kitchen when I am on the phone, those were the only times she said she loved him, as far as I can remember, not that she was gushing with love for any of the boys, not until Evan came along, somehow she softened up when it came to Evan, it was like she needed three practice sons to figure it out, she finally got it right with Evan, I'm not complaining, I was all right, growing up I mainly wanted to stay out of the way of Adam and Willie, I didn't want to aggravate Mom any more than I had to, I kept my head down, it wasn't ideal but it was easier to do it that way, keep your head down, in any case Carl suggested that we take the gun out for a spin, that was his phrase, what do you say we take this pistol out for a spin, so we made our way slowly out of the house and around the back, where they sometimes did target shooting, and he set up some cans on a rock at the far end of a small field, he had Adam's gun and Mom had a rifle of some sort, it was a shotgun, I guess, and they both had headphones, they needed to protect their ears, they said, and Carl stood erect and fired Adam's handgun at the can, but he missed, it's a pretty decent kickback, he said, Cary, do you want to try it, but she shook her head and put the shotgun to her shoulder and pulled the trigger, once, twice, and the can jumped in the air and shredded, she was a good shot, she blasted it right off the rock just with the two shots, she knew how to shoot, Carl had taught her that, she had a crabbed way of walking and she coughed a lot, that was the cigarettes, but she knew how to handle a gun, I guess, and she said, when Adam told me he had a gun, well, I told him I had a gun too

That was why, I thought, my mother didn't much care about having a memorial service for Adam, why would she care about a memorial service for him, since he had threatened to kill her, it had taken two years before she agreed to take part, she finally thought it was the right time, two years after the fact, she could blame the delay on the pandemic, it was true we had to wait during the pandemic, but that really wasn't the reason for the delay, she just didn't want to do it, she didn't have any interest, she finally agreed, I think Carl must have persuaded her, God knows it wasn't Evan, he didn't care about a service either, I had to push them all, they needed me to arrange the service, I suppose I could have held it without them, but that seemed sad, even Adam didn't deserve that, and now that we had gathered in the meeting room at the Amory Public Library I could see that my mother was glad she had come, she was chatting with some of her old friends and neighbors from Amory, maybe she had been like me, worried that no one would be there, just a few family members, there were so few of us left, but there were more than twenty people in the room now, and half the family members weren't even there yet, it was only a few minutes before eleven but Evan wasn't there yet, neither were Daphne and Muriel, they were sending texts, they were close, but they weren't there yet, it didn't matter, I still wasn't sure what to say about Adam, and Julia wasn't there yet either, maybe she wouldn't come, I thought, and that would be better,

I thought, to be honest it would be better if she didn't come, I had been to funerals where relatives and survivors settled scores, sometimes bad blood came out at memorial services, it would be better if I stood up and said a few nice words about Adam, and Daphne had found a poem to read, she barely knew Adam but she wanted to read a poem, and if Julia wanted to read her statement, if she wanted to blame us, Adam's family, for his death, well, we would just have to sit through it, although myself I didn't see the point, what was the purpose, why open old wounds, as the saying goes, why dig up dirt, another old saying, or air dirty laundry, there are a lot of clichés, but the clichés were right, there was no point in airing dirty laundry or opening old wounds, they only felt fresh that morning in the meeting room at the Amory Public Library because we were there to remember Adam, or maybe, for some of us, we were there to complete our memories of him, to *stop* remembering him, yes, actually, if I had my way, I would give my eulogy, and Daphne would read a poem, and we would remember Adam for a few minutes, and that would be that, the memories would stop, that would be the end of it, although of course I knew it wouldn't work that way, and there was still the question of Julia Slotkin, if she read her statement out loud, if she decided to speak off the cuff it would be even worse, probably, either way, we would go on thinking about Adam, we would go on thinking about him forever, that's the fact of it, we try to set things aside, we try to forget difficulties, we have ceremonies like memorial services, they're not meant for remembering, they're mainly meant to help us stop remembering, to mark an end of remembering, but it makes no difference, we just keep remembering, no matter how much we would like the remembering to cease

After that trip to Vermont, when Mom showed me how she could handle a gun, I called Julia again, this time to offer her some of Adam's things, because no one else wanted them, there were just three or four boxes, my mother didn't want anything, Evan didn't want anything, I didn't want anything, that was the family, that was all of us, but maybe Julia would want something, and that would give me a chance to ask her about Adam's state of mind, maybe she had an idea of what had happened to Adam on the last night, I wasn't sure she would talk because our conversations had been tense and short, but she agreed to meet me, she seemed interested in looking through the things I had saved from Adam's apartment, she told me she had come by the apartment and tried to get in, but she didn't have a key, I suppose she and Adam hadn't gotten to that point in their relationship yet, it was an odd kind of relationship, but anyway, they didn't have each other's keys, and when she learned that Adam had died, she learned this from the local news, apparently, Dead Man Found in Canal Identified, that was the headline on the local news site, she did try to get into the apartment, how she thought she would get in I don't know, but she came over to the Treadway apartment building and tried to get into Adam's place, but couldn't, I didn't tell Julia I knew, I knew that she had done that, because the old woman next door to Adam's had said to me, did you find the girl, so I knew she had tried to get in, and I felt encouraged that she was honest with me about having gone there, basically she would have been trespassing, not that I would have cared, really, not that anyone would have cared, to be honest Julia was probably the only person in the world who would have cared about someone trespassing in Adam's apartment, in fact she sort of saw my presence in the apartment as trespassing, she felt I didn't belong there, I didn't deserve to be there, in her mind I had abandoned Adam, I had ignored him at a time when he needed me, it hurt me to hear that, of course, because a part of me saw it that way, too, a part of me felt guilty that I had not called Adam, I had only called him that one time at the beginning of the lockdown, although I didn't know how I could have made the trip from Los Angeles, at least in the early part of the pandemic, but I could have called more than the one time, I could have called him back, so, yes, when she accused me of ignoring Adam at an important moment of his life, I didn't push back, she wasn't wrong, she didn't know the history, or understand how difficult Adam had been all my life, more than difficult, how awful he had been, I didn't tell her how frightened I had been of him as a child, I didn't mention that once, hearing him behind me in the hall in middle school, I had panicked and wet my pants, that was how terrified Adam had made me when I was a child, a part of me wanted to grab her arm and tell her, listen, you have no idea, you have no idea how hard it was for me to interact with him as an adult, he never reached out to me, I was always the one to reach out to him, and even then, I had to put up with his paternalism, his condescension, that was the word, he was condescending, he had a way of worming information out of me, he could always find a way to get me to tell him how much I was earning, and I wasn't going to get into the last time I had seen him, the time when he suggested that Muriel was not my actual biological child, he knew how to bore into your private fears, he knew enough about my complicated relationship with Daphne and Jeremy, I wasn't going to get into any of that with Julia of course, but it was tempting, oh, it was tempting, to say, well, here are the sorts of things he did, you want to hear about what your special friend did to me, your special friend, that was the phrase she had used to describe her relationship with Adam, her special friend, they were special friends, I think because they were not in any kind of identifiable relationship, they were not boyfriend and girlfriend, I don't think they were having sex, I don't know, what does it matter, but she never referred to him as her boyfriend, let alone her fiancé, it wasn't like they had talked about getting married, although that phrase, special friend, it sounded funny to me, it reminded me of *The Big Lebowski*, my special lady, it was just about the only thing that was halfway amusing about any of this, Julia calling Adam her special friend, but it wasn't that funny, really, it was sad, she meant it unironically, she wasn't thinking of *The Big Lebowski*, she really meant that he was her special friend

I drove those last four boxes back to Connecticut, I was driving those boxes all over New England, I was trying to figure out what to do with them, I knew it was silly of me but the longer I had his things, the more I wanted to find someone who would want at least something of Adam's belongings, Evan and I had thrown away all but four boxes, my mother hadn't wanted anything, she said she had her memories of Adam, that was enough, but what she was saying was really the opposite, she was saying she didn't want memories of Adam, I couldn't blame her, really, after all, he had threatened her over the phone, not that I believed he would have done anything, and speaking of the gun, I still had it, I originally had thought I would leave it with Carl, since he liked shooting skeet and shooting at cans and stumps, he called it plinking, anyway, I had thought it would make sense to leave Adam's gun with Carl, but it seemed strange to do that after I learned that Adam had threatened to shoot Mom, again, I didn't think he would have done it, but still he had made the threat, anyway, Mom claimed that he had threatened her, so it wasn't right to ask Carl to keep a gun that had been part of a threat to his wife, and I was more comfortable carrying it around, because Carl had removed the cartridge, there weren't any bullets anymore, so the gun was in one of the boxes, along with some books and some personal belongings, the belongings, well, for instance, there were datebooks, Adam had kept all of his datebooks, leather-bound datebooks,

I remembered he had gotten one when he was still in college, it struck me as pretentious then, but he had kept notes there, meetings, that sort of thing, it was old-fashioned, it seemed like he had never kept an electronic calendar, I guess he was just old enough to have gotten started in his professional life when businessmen still kept datebooks, so I had them, there were twenty-eight of them in all, he had kept them all through the years, so those were the personal belongings I kept, the datebooks, some photo albums, the gun, a few more things, it wasn't really enough to fill the four boxes, I probably could have repacked them down, maybe I could have even compressed it to two boxes, that was how few things I had kept out of his apartment in Ogden, and even among these very few items, no one seemed to want anything, Evan hadn't wanted even a single book or photo, and Mom hadn't wanted anything, maybe if Adam had kept a lot of photos, but he didn't, there were hardly any, the pages of the photo albums were mostly empty, a few childhood pictures, some news articles from the high school paper, a page or two of photos of his ex-wife, Celeste, from the days he lived in Greenwich, the mansion in Greenwich, it was a brief marriage, and speaking of her I wondered if Celeste had considered coming to this memorial service, most likely not, since it had been such a bitter divorce, and the marriage had been so brief, it had been a long time ago, still, I had managed to find an address for her and sent a note, but I didn't hear back, in any case Celeste wouldn't want any of this stuff, so I called Julia again, I said I was driving through Connecticut again, would she like to meet me, I would like to meet her, I said, and if she wanted a keepsake of some sort, I had a few boxes of Adam's belongings, I would be happy for her to have something to remember Adam by, honestly, thinking to myself I would be happy for her to take all four boxes, I didn't want anything myself, I just didn't feel comfortable throwing the last few things away, so if Julia had said she wanted it all, the datebooks, the albums, even the gun, I would have given it all to her, the only thing left of Adam's life would be his car, I was driving his car around New England, up to Vermont to visit my mother and back to Connecticut to finish off the job of closing his apartment and disposing of his belongings, I was down to four boxes and the car, that was it, four boxes and a car, and Julia agreed to meet me in Milford, where she lived, it was near to Ogden, near to Adam's old apartment, the next town over, she agreed to meet on the town square

She was distrustful, she didn't want to meet at her home, and it was Covid days, so we wouldn't want to sit across from each other in a restaurant, it was better to meet outside somewhere, she suggested the town square in Milford, she said I would see her, she had orange hair, by which it turned out she meant that she had dyed her hair orange, it was brilliant orange, like yarn, sitting in my car by the edge of the town square I could see her across the lawn, a slash of orange, oh, I thought, she has orange hair, which was just as she told me she would, but I imagined that she meant she was a redhead, a strawberry blonde, that sort of thing, but no, it was orange, and she was tall, you could see her from a distance because of her height and the color of her hair, she stood out, and I let myself out of my car and gestured to her, I could see that she noticed me but it was strange, she didn't wave back or nod to me, she just continued walking, and when she had crossed the park she stopped about ten feet from me, that was Covid, you were supposed to stand six feet apart, she wasn't taking any chances with me, she had a mask around her neck, ready to pull up if necessary, I had a mask, too, looped over my wrist, and finally she asked me what I wanted, that's actually what she said, what do you want, but before I could answer she told me, wait, and she took a phone from her purse and held it up, she was recording our conversation, and I told her that I had a few belongings that she might be interested in, the datebooks, a scrapbook, and I said, it's weird, there's a gun in there too, I found a gun in his apartment, I haven't been sure what to do with it, I was going to give it to the police, turn it in, I think you can do that, but the police have been so busy, so I'm just carrying it around right now, I'll have to get rid of it somehow, well, I was running on at the mouth, it was unnerving to have her filming me that way, recording what I was saying, and when I was done she said, I have some questions for you, yes, she was brusque like that, she just spat the words at me, I have some questions for you, in any case the first thing she wanted to know was when was the last time I had spoken to Adam, so I told her about my call, I had phoned him just at the beginning of the pandemic, when everything was shutting down, when everyone stayed home, he was sick, I told her, well, I said, Adam *had been* sick but he was feeling better when I spoke with him, I phrased it that way out of guilt, of course, I could have called him back later, I should have, but I didn't, it was so exhausting to deal with Adam, at the time I just felt like I had done my duty, I had called him, I had made contact, that was what I had done, he never called me back, he never reached out, thinking back on the conversation with Julia, I suppose I wasn't completely honest, no, I wasn't completely transparent, I told her the truth but I left out the rest, I had worried about calling him back but I couldn't bring myself to do it, anyway, she was surprised I had called him at all, she was under the impression I had not called him since my Hollywood breakthrough, that was her phrase, she was speaking sarcastically, your Hollywood breakthrough, Adam had told her about *Catbirds*, or, well, he always had been mixed-up about *Catbirds*, or he purposely misremembered it, I had told him so many times I hadn't made much money from that movie, besides, I barely had anything to do with it, it was my story originally but Jeremy completely rewrote it, whatever,

it was done, Adam couldn't get it out of his head, and now
Julia had the same misunderstanding, so I tried to explain it
to her but I could see from the expression on her face she was
skeptical, she was scowling as I told her about Willie and the
rest of us, and Terry, and the story of "Catbirds," the story I
wrote, not the movie, the story of the four of us brothers, Adam
and Willie and me and Evan, or the five of us, counting Terry,
the half brother who had no place in the family, my mother had
no patience for Terry, she should have been kinder to Terry,
but as it was she was dealing with her own sons, in her way
she was dealing with her own sons, and Julia stopped me and
she said, wait, she said, who is Terry

Standing a bit aside from the doorway of the Amory Public Library, I remembered how surprised Julia had been to hear the name Terry, she had not heard about him, she had thought she knew everything about our family, and she did actually know quite a lot, for instance, she knew about my mother's smoking, she knew about Evan, she knew he was much younger, of course she knew about Willie, and she knew about the park behind our house, she knew we called it Short Park, she even knew why we called it Short Park, and she even described it, she described it as a pretty wooded area, even though she had never been there, it was strange to hear her describing, so warmly, a place she had never been, or at least as far as I knew she had never been there, and of course she knew that Adam had gone to Yale, his great triumph, and she knew my father had worked as an accountant and that his main client had been the university, she knew about his Huntington's and that my parents were divorced by the time he died, she knew a lot about us, although it was cockeyed, for instance she thought I was wealthy because of *Catbirds*, not only that, she thought that Evan was a janitor, which wasn't the case, he was the facilities manager for a small museum and botanical garden, he had started in maintenance, he had never left, now he managed the entire facility, but she thought he was a janitor, in any case she knew a lot about us, and she misunderstood a fair amount, but she had never heard that there was another brother, the oldest

of us, our half brother, Terry, and after I explained who he was
she thought about it for a moment and asked me if I was telling
the truth, and I said, why would I make something like that up,
of course I was telling the truth, but for some reason she found
it hard to believe that Adam had a half brother, why wouldn't
he have told me about that, she said to me, although she wasn't
asking me a question, she was saying it out loud to herself, she
was shaken by the information, and she put her phone in her
bag, I don't know if she was still recording our conversation
anymore, and she said, so there were even more of you who
didn't visit him, there were *three* brothers who abandoned him,
not just you and Evan, and it was strange, it was strange the
way she referred to Evan as if she knew him, and she said,
you abandoned him and Evan abandoned him, and even his
half brother abandoned him, all of you abandoned him, and I
wasn't sure what to say to that because it was actually true, she
was right, that Evan had essentially abandoned Adam, Evan
was seven years younger than Adam, he never knew him very
well, but he knew enough to stay out of Adam's way, if he did
something that upset Adam, Adam could hold Evan down
with one hand, he was much stronger and bigger, he had done
that, he had held Evan down and hissed, stay out of my room,
stay out of my stuff, Evan had found some pornography in
there, I don't remember what it was, and Adam caught him
and pushed him down on the floor and held him there with one
hand, I saw it, I was on the stairway, I froze up, I'm ashamed,
I froze up when I saw Adam holding Evan down that way, it
reminded me of the way that Adam and Willie had fought, all
those years of fighting I had ducked back, I had stayed out of
it, stayed out of the fray, and now, I saw, it was starting again,
only with Evan, who was so much smaller than us, and besides,
Evan wasn't fierce like Willie, he wasn't going to fight back, he

wasn't going to sharpen two pencils and hold them secretly in either hand to stab Adam, he didn't have that kind of temper, he was more of a kind of spacey kid, spacey but aware of the fact that you had to stay out of Adam's way, it was surprising that he had gone into Adam's room, I guess pictures of naked women were interesting enough to draw him in there, I had probably been the one to blab to him about it, Adam had a bunch of magazines, I don't know where he got them, it was before internet porn, anyway, when I saw Adam holding Evan down I wasn't able to make myself do anything about it, I might have if Adam had hit Evan, maybe I would have run at him, I hope I would have, but Adam didn't actually hit Evan, he just held him down, and when he loosed his grip on Evan's shirt, I edged down the stairs, for once the steps didn't creak as I backstepped down the stairs, out of sight, I don't think either of them saw me there, anyway, I thought of that afternoon when Julia said that Evan had abandoned Adam, that was the thing I thought of, Adam holding Evan down, helpless, in the hallway outside his room, and me standing just below them, mostly out of sight, on the stairs up from the living room, and I remembered the look on Evan's face, and I thought, yes, Evan abandoned Adam, he had always hated Adam, when we were cleaning out Adam's apartment together, Evan told me that when he was a kid he had imagined the ways he would kill Adam, for instance he imagined throwing an electric toaster into the bathtub with Adam, that was how he imagined killing him as a boy, so it was no wonder that Evan would abandon Adam, although it was also true, I thought, when Julia said that we had all abandoned Adam, that Adam had never bothered to stay in contact with us, in fact he had abandoned us, you might say, but again I didn't tell that to Julia, I just thought it was true that Evan had never wanted anything to do with

Adam, even in childhood and especially as an adult, and Willie was dead, of course, and Dad had died, then there was Mom, Mom was Mom, she just didn't get along with Adam, so none of them were in contact with Adam, but I was, I thought, I didn't say it but I thought it, I was in contact with him, I had called Adam occasionally, he didn't call me, I called him, but Julia was hung up on the idea that there was even *another* brother, Terry, another family member who had spurned Adam, and I could have tried to explain it to her, Terry wasn't around much, he was on the spectrum, none of us had known him, really, when we were growing up, I didn't tell her any of that, what was the point, she had learned about us from Adam, I could only imagine what Julia must think about us, based on whatever Adam had said, but she surprised me, she said she had just one question for me, there was just one thing she wanted to know, and she narrowed her eyes before she asked me, like she was observing me closely to see if I would lie, she said, tell me the truth, she said, do you work for the government

I was confused, when she asked if I worked for the government, and I said, well, I used to work for the Los Angeles County school system, but that was just an internship, and Julia said, no, she snapped at me, no, that's not what I'm talking about, I'm asking if you work for the CIA, that was what she said, did I work for the CIA, and I said, what, what are you talking about, and she said, I know that you worked with him on a case, and I said, no, Julia, no, I do not work for the CIA, and neither did Adam, if he told you he worked for the CIA that wasn't true, and she said, well, that's why he had the gun, she believed that he had worked on a case for the CIA, Adam had told her he worked for the CIA and that was why he had a gun, and I laughed out loud, I didn't mean to but I laughed out loud, which Julia didn't like, she glared at me and told me he needed the gun for protection, it all went back to the securities firm he had worked for years and years ago, it had all been a front, she told me, it was a money-laundering operation, there was drug smuggling and gun smuggling involved, so Adam needed a gun, he had been issued the gun, and that was the reason he needed protection, the government had drafted him to help with the investigation, and I stopped her and I said, Julia, none of that is true, I don't have anything to do with the CIA, I'm just a therapist, and Adam never worked for the CIA either, but Julia didn't really seem to believe me, she shook her head, she said I misunderstood, she had never said, Adam had never said, that he worked for the CIA, she said, no, she said, Adam was doing it to help them, that was all, so I stopped her again, I held up my hands and I told her again that I had never had anything to do with the CIA, and as far as I knew, Adam hadn't either, and she said something about nondisclosure agreements, secrecy, of course there wouldn't be a paper trail, and then she stopped and said something about Julia Roberts, she said, what about Julia Roberts, and of course I said what about her, and she said, again, Julia Roberts, after the movie, what movie, I said, *Catbirds*, she said, Adam got to know Julia Roberts during the filming of *Catbirds*, and she told me how they had gotten to know one another, they had actually snuck out of a mall together, there had been a security situation in a mall, and he had helped her out a service entrance, it had been a close call, but he had managed to get Julia Roberts out in one piece, and at this point I suppose I stopped paying attention, I just stopped taking it all in, I could only look at this woman, Julia Slotkin, who had been my brother's only friend, apparently she had been his only friend, and she believed that Adam had been involved in CIA operations and that he had been friendly with a movie star, and somehow I was the nexus of all this, the CIA and Hollywood, and I thought back, I calculated that it had been three years between the time I last saw Adam and the time he died, I had spoken to him on the phone just the one time, when the Covid lockdowns began, it had been three years, I didn't feel good thinking about that, but I reminded myself what a prick Adam had been to me, not just in childhood but throughout my life, still, I had been a lousy brother to him, and while I was thinking about all of that I halfway heard Julia saying something about diabetes treatments and my mother, and I stopped her and asked her to repeat herself, and she said that Adam had called my mother to

ask for money to pay for a diabetes treatment, but my mother
had turned him down, and it wasn't just diabetes, it was a lot
of other things, he was having trouble sleeping, he had cloudy
vision, and Julia herself had tried to help, she had sleeping pills,
they had experimented together with some of her prescription
medications, but nothing seemed to help, nothing helped, he
needed money, he needed better insurance, and no one would
help him, and my mother, Julia said, had told Adam to go to
hell, yes, Julia said, your mother told him to go to hell, and
Julia's breathing sped up, she actually began to pant when she
told me that Mom had told Adam to go to hell, so, she said,
that was when we drove up to Vermont, to get money from
your mother, we had to have money for his medical treatments,
so we drove to Vermont to get the money from your mother

I said to Julia, wait, you went to Vermont to get money from my mother, and she nodded, she said yes, they had driven up to Vermont, they had followed 91 almost to St. Johnsbury, Julia was driving because Adam couldn't see well in the dark, he couldn't drive at night anymore, and the farther north they drove, the more unhinged Adam had become, at one point he was crying, his family had betrayed him, they had lied to him, they had left him alone and helpless, he was rocking back and forth, she was worried he would actually collide with her in the driver's seat, ram into her while she was driving, so she had to pull off, and they came to a stop in the emergency lane, and Adam screamed at her, keep going, don't fucking stop, I'm going to kill that bitch, and he dug in the backpack on the floor and pulled out a gun, and he snapped something, Julia said, he pulled on something on the gun and it made a snapping sound, and he said, I'm finally going to do it, I'll shoot her, she's killing me, but I'm going to kill her before she does, and Julia froze in terror, she wanted to run away but her legs wouldn't work, she said, don't do that, don't talk like that, and Adam wailed and banged his head against the passenger window, hard enough she thought that the glass might break, and he cried for what must have been five minutes, sobbing, gasping for air, moaning, and finally Julia put out her hand and asked him to give her the gun, and he did, he gave it to her, and she sat there with the gun in her hand while Adam's breath calmed down, and a minute later he was asleep, he was deep asleep, he was *snoring*, Julia told me, she couldn't quite understand what had happened or why he had suddenly fallen asleep, but she didn't know if the gun was loaded or how it worked, she didn't know what the snapping sound had been when he had been waving it around, she was frightened, at first she thought she would just throw the gun into the grass by the highway, but there would be fingerprints, so she slid it into the compartment on the driver's door at her side, she wedged it down with a knit cap she had been wearing, so the gun wouldn't rattle around or go off, and she drove to the next exit, where she turned around and drove them back to Connecticut, they had been less than half an hour from Mom's house when they turned back, it had been that close

Julia and I stood in silence at the edge of the grass of the town square, it was hot, the streets were quiet, you would hardly know there had been marches and clashes with police just a few days ago, you wouldn't have known that the town, the whole country, was dealing with a pandemic, there were a hundred thousand dead at that point, and she touched her dyed-orange hair nervously and didn't say anything for a moment, then her eyes lit on something beyond me, she said, that was our favorite place to have breakfast, that restaurant, and she pointed to an old-style diner a couple blocks away, a silver diner, it's closed now because of the pandemic, she said, I guess they didn't want to do takeout, and I said, I didn't know what else to say, I asked Julia, did Adam have a favorite breakfast order, what was his favorite breakfast, and she looked at me in a kind of horror, don't you know, she asked me, don't you know what your brother liked for breakfast, I shook my head, no, I didn't know, and I said, there's a lot of things I don't know about Adam, I don't know what he did for money for the last five or six years, I don't know what happened to his condo in Norwalk, I don't know what he ate for breakfast or dinner or lunch, we were never close, really, we had a combative relationship, I had tried to keep in contact with him but he made it difficult, he was patronizing, he had a hair-trigger temper, he was arrogant, he was impossible to be with, so I don't know what he had for breakfast, I can tell you he didn't like it if you put a lemon

wedge in his vodka tonic, at least I know that much, that was
what I said to Julia, I ran on at the mouth a little, I don't
remember everything I said to her, I just, as they say, let it out,
I hadn't really let it out before, not that I was screaming at her,
but how was I to know what Adam's favorite breakfast was,
I said to Julia, he had never invited me to spend a night with
him, even in high school, when I was in high school and he was
a college freshman, he never suggested I come visit his dorm,
his college, as he called it, he referred to his dorm as his college,
it's a Yale thing, the dorms are called colleges, whatever, I knew
plenty of kids whose older brothers invited them to visit, Adam
never did, not that I would have taken him up on it, of course
not, I had no interest in spending time with him, I had been
grateful he was gone from the house, it was a different world
without him there, although it wasn't a long period of peace,
Willie came down sick and then died, Mom and Dad split up,
it all happened in the space of a few years, one explosion or
another, and then it was all gone, my mother remarried and
living farther north in Connecticut, my father in an apartment
in New Haven, and my college roommate, Jeremy, my best
friend, we had made some student films together, he said, let's
go to California after we graduate, I've got a car, you can pay for
gas, so I left, I drove away with Jeremy, Mom and Dad weren't
divorced yet but they would be soon, as soon as Evan went
to college, the next year, by then I was living in Los Angeles,
Jeremy and I were sharing an apartment, we had left everything
behind, our families, all that history, so, I thought, how could
I have known what Adam ate for breakfast, how could I have
known anything about him, the two of us had bailed out of
the family as soon as we could, he bailed out, I bailed out, I
was different, I tried to stay in touch, I came back east once
every year or so, but he didn't invite me to visit, I didn't always

stop by, I would go to see Mom and Dad, Dad before he died, sometimes Evan, it was an effort to see Adam, he was always busy, more than once he couldn't make time to see me when I called up and suggested we have lunch or dinner, it was like scheduling a business appointment, so, no, I said, I didn't know what Adam ate for breakfast, and Julia said, in a quiet voice, Western omelet, she said, Western omelet with extra ham on the side and whole wheat toast

Well, I didn't know what Adam's favorite breakfast order was, I said, but I remembered when we were kids, I remembered eating cereal, Fruity Pebbles, I said, he ate Fruity Pebbles, when we were growing up, Fruity Pebbles was his favorite cereal, we all wanted the Fruity Pebbles, we were always running out of it before the other cereals, Adam used to run down the stairs to get first crack at it, that was his favorite cereal, and Julia seemed interested to hear this fact, something she had not known about Adam, and so I told her more, I said, *stampede*, I told her how he barreled around the house, I didn't tell her that he had terrorized me with that word, I didn't tell her, of course I didn't tell her, that he had once caused me to wet my pants, my first day of middle school, *stampede*, the panic it caused me, no, I didn't tell her that part of it, I just told her the way he had hollered it, *stampede*, when he ran down the stairs, or when my mother had called out the back door, *dinner*, she never cared much for cooking but we were boys, we ate anything, we were constantly hungry, *dinner*, my mother would call, and most nights we came tearing back to the house, we liked to chase around the woods behind the house, Short Park, it wasn't really woods, it was trees and a creek, but it was directly behind our house, it was like our woods, and we played out there, yes, Adam, yes, and Willie, we played out there, we played tag, we played hide and seek, *ollie-ollie-oxen-free*, Willie and Adam and me, Willie liked to wear a cape, we didn't care, we played Star Wars, we had plastic light sabers, *bzoom bzoom*, we fired imaginary guns at each other, *pew pew pew*, I forgot, I said, I forgot how much we played, even with Willie we played, he would dress up in Mom's clothes but he played in the woods with us, sometimes he ran around in her clothes in the woods, I forgot, we didn't really care, he could be Princess Leia, we played that way, Evan was too little, dinner, my mother would call, and we tripped over ourselves to get back to the house, there was Evan in a playpen while my mother finished putting the meal on the table, my father didn't help, he was old-fashioned, he was considerably older, *stampede*, Adam cried out, and we ran inside for dinner, don't eat like animals, my mother would say, tell me what happened in the woods, my father would say, he always asked about the woods, he never went there himself, he didn't even mow the lawn, he paid someone to do it, later on he paid Adam to do it, and then me, I suppose Evan must have done it after that, I had never seen my father mow the lawn or hammer a nail, he worked with papers and pencils and a pocket calculator, he wasn't handy around the house, as they say, he barely owned any tools, my mother had a small toolbox, my father called it that, your mother's toolbox, he didn't open it, he didn't use her tools, and he didn't go in the woods, I can hardly remember him even going down the steps to the backyard from the porch, he stayed on the porch reading the newspaper or working with his papers and pencil and calculator, but at dinner he would ask what we had done in the woods, did we find frogs, did we play tag, did we play cowboys and Indians, *Dad*, we said, no one plays cowboys and Indians, well I did, he said, when I was a kid we played cowboys and Indians, we played war games, we played with toy soldiers, we set up battlefields, we spent hours arranging toy soldiers on the ground, we thought about war all the time, did you know that, he asked us, did you know we thought that Russia was going to drop a bomb on us, we used to get under our desks for bomb drills, and the school had tunnels downstairs, there were basements with food and blankets, we used to sneak down there, believe it or not, we broke into the bomb shelters and we ate the hard candies down there, there were lemon candies, *Dad stole candy*, we cried, we could not imagine him breaking into a bomb shelter to steal candy, lemon drops, not our accountant dad, it was impossible to imagine, our gawky father, a father who barely went out in the yard, who never stopped working, even after dinner he would go back to his papers and his calculator, he barely watched TV, on Friday nights my mother liked to watch *Dallas*, we all had to be in bed by ten so she could watch *Dallas*, but my father didn't watch, he looked at newspapers or books while my mother watched, he couldn't keep the characters straight, he didn't really have interests, hobbies, he read mystery novels, he read science fiction, I suppose that was his hobby, and he liked to hear what we did out back, in the woods, he always wanted to hear what went on back there, *tadpoles in the creek*, he said, I *wouldn't mind hearing more about that*, as if we were explorers or astronauts, reporting back from some distant place, it was just out the back door but I don't know if he ever went into the park, it was enough for us to tell him about it, I told Julia, our father was satisfied just to hear about the world out there beyond the backyard, and when it was dinnertime, I told Julia, we ran inside, we were starving, *stampede*, Adam used to shout, running through the dark of the woods, back toward the dim light of our backyard, and what about your mother, Julia said, she wasn't a good cook, was she, Adam must have told her, I guess, that my mother was not a good cook, no, I said, terrible, she hated cooking, but none of us cared, we ate whatever she served, we barely ate vegetables, we had iceberg lettuce with Italian dressing, Wish-Bone, we had it every night, we had hamburgers and hot dogs, we had frozen french fries, Adam's favorite dinner was meat loaf, when he was seven or eight I remember he ate three full slabs, you're going to be sick, my mother said, but he wasn't, he loved meat loaf, we all loved spaghetti, we went to an Italian restaurant once every couple weeks, we had pizza and spaghetti, Evan sat in a high chair by Mom, while Adam and Willie and I played dots, the tablecloth was a piece of paper with crayons, every time we would set up a grid and play dots with crayons, that was what we did in the Italian restaurant, we played dots, we loved the pizza there, and when Evan was just a baby Mom would give him strands of spaghetti with butter and he would slurp them up, it was hilarious, we would shriek with laughter, *do it again, do it again, give him more spaghetti, Mom, slurp up another noodle, Evan,* it got Willie laughing so hard once that he fell off his chair, and Adam laughed until he cried

Julia smiled, imagining, I guess, the idea of Adam laughing so hard while my mother fed lengths of spaghetti into little Evan's mouth, and then she said, that's why you called it "Catbirds," wasn't it, because of your mother feeding the children that way, like a mother bird, and I nodded, I pretended that was right but that was not it at all, that was not why I had chosen that title, no, actually Mom had called us that, *catbirds*, she said, *you're screeching like catbirds*, she would say when we were bickering in the back seat of the car, and then, years later, I read something about catbird behavior, apparently catbirds recognize when other birds try to sneak eggs into their nests, when that happens they attack the eggs, they destroy them, they pierce the shells and eject them from the nest, but I told Julia, yes, yes, I called it "Catbirds" because of the way my mom had fed Evan spaghetti

Well, I said, what happened after you turned the car around, after you drove almost all the way to my mother's house in Vermont, did you just drive straight home again, and she said yes, that was what she had done, Adam was asleep, he was snoring loudly, like some kind of wild animal, it was frightening, and meanwhile she couldn't stop thinking about the gun, the gun was in the compartment at her side, she worried that he might lunge for it when he woke up, but he didn't wake up, he just kept snoring, she had never heard anything quite like the sound he was making, he moaned as he exhaled, and the sound of him breathing in was like a drill, like a motorcycle with a bad muffler, it sounded painful, she said, like something dragging through him, and then he would moan, as if he couldn't withstand another inhalation, but after maybe half an hour his breathing eased, maybe he changed positions, she wished she could lower his seat so that he could curl up a little, she wanted to give him some sense of ease, really that was all she had ever wanted, she told me, she wanted to ease his mind, he was so anguished, she said, she had never seen someone so full of anguish, he had lost everything, his home, his career, his family, he had lost his money, he had once had a great deal of money but it was gone, it had been taken from him by unscrupulous former business partners, the smugglers, his own lawyers never had his best interests at heart, and there was a judge who had screwed him over completely, he knew he could fight back, there were channels, there were appeals, he had some new lawyers in mind, but his health was failing him, he couldn't sleep, he couldn't concentrate, he needed help, and she tried to help, they tried her meds, she had gone through some similar issues, and of course I knew that but I didn't say anything, I had seen her prescriptions in his cabinet, that was why they were there, he was taking pills that had been prescribed to her, but even when he managed to get some sleep, she told me, his other physical problems were getting worse, it was harder to walk, it was painful, he had painful pins and needles, they both knew what that meant, and his sight was going, and they knew what that meant too, that was why they needed the money from my mother, that was why they had driven to Vermont, but she didn't understand, she didn't realize he was bringing a gun, she knew how cruel my mother had been, she said, she knew how hateful my mother had always been to Adam, she said, but it hadn't occurred to her that Adam would bring a gun, that he would think to hold his own mother at gunpoint, how could she have known that Adam would do such a thing, the Adam she knew was gentle and anguished, but he was losing hope, he needed hope, he needed money, his mother, *our* mother, wouldn't talk to him on the phone, she would hang up on him, he needed to speak to her in person, and Julia knew he shouldn't drive, so she drove him, she was happy to do that for him, it was the least she could do, she didn't have much money either but she could drive him to Vermont so that he could get money for the medical care he needed

But what happened *afterward*, I asked, after he waved the gun around in the car, after she had turned off the highway and got back on 91 going south, back toward Massachusetts and Connecticut, what happened when she had driven him home, did they go to his apartment, I asked, did they go to her apartment, I had been trying to piece together Adam's last days, how long before Adam went missing, I asked her, did she know, but she shook her head a little, she didn't know, and the reason, she admitted to me, was that she was scared, she was freaked out, naturally she was freaked out by Adam waving a gun in the car, so she had driven him home, she got him to bed, it was like he was drunk, or maybe hungover, he couldn't speak clearly, his steps were uncertain, she got him into bed, and when he was asleep she hid the gun in a bureau drawer under a pile of shirts, there were so many there, she thought he might not notice, she didn't even like to touch the gun, she said, repeating that in Vermont Adam had done something to the gun that made a snapping sound, it was loaded or cocked, she didn't really know, maybe the safety was off, she didn't know anything about guns, she didn't want to know anything about guns, it didn't matter how cruel his mother had been, my mother, *our* mother, Julia hadn't expected Adam to threaten his mother with a gun, she hadn't considered anything like that, and then the sound of him sleeping, that had freaked her out as well, the animal sounds he had made, so she left him at home, and after that they only talked once or twice, they didn't see each other in person because they had heard about this thing, a disease, in China, it was a virus, it was killing people, and then it came to the United States, it somehow spread across the world like wildfire, and she was afraid to go out, they said it was worse for people with immune system disorders, she had immunity issues, so she stayed inside, she stayed home, and what about Adam, I asked, I don't know, she said, I'm not sure, he needed to stay safe too, and also I was afraid of him, I was afraid of him after the trip to Vermont, waving the gun around, falling asleep all of a sudden, the groaning and the snoring, I was afraid of him, I shouldn't have been, he needed me, he needed someone, everyone in the family had abandoned him, and the government wouldn't give him what he was owed, but I was afraid, I was afraid of getting sick and I was afraid of your poor brother, I shouldn't have been but I was, I should have kept that gun, maybe I wouldn't have been afraid of him if I had taken the gun home, but I was afraid of the gun, so I left it, she said, I didn't see him again, she said, I never saw him again

So in the end, I thought, standing near the doorway of the
meeting room in the Amory Public Library, Adam really had
been alone, he had frightened poor Julia Slotkin, she hadn't
known what she was getting into when she became friends
with Adam, friends, lovers, I wasn't sure, it was never clear,
she referred to him as a cherished friend, her special friend,
she called him that, who knows what she meant by that, it
didn't matter either way, it didn't matter if she and Adam had
been a couple or just friends, either way it didn't matter, by
the time they befriended one another he was delusional, she
had believed that Adam had helped Julia Roberts escape a
mob scene at a mall, I had to smile at that, and something
about a government investigation, and my involvement in it,
he was deluded at the end, his body was falling apart, and he
was alone, and he was broke, behind on his rent, late on the
car, he needed money, I never asked my mother how much he
had wanted, maybe he never told her, I have no idea what he
was asking for, he had been asking me for money, I knew that
now, but I didn't pick that up at the time, I thought it was
some cockamamie investment scheme he had come up with,
he had been close to broke for two or three years, he had won
a small settlement in a dispute with a former partner, that had
kept him going for a while, but he seemed to have forgotten
how to work, that was the amazing thing, that he would have
stopped working, that was what Adam was good at, working,

maybe he felt he couldn't find a job that was suitable to his vision of himself, I could see that, although at the end he was living in the Treadway, he was living in an apartment building among dusty strip malls, there was a tire shop across the street, what sort of vision did he have of himself at the end, he could have done something, he was so dogged, I don't know, it's hard to know, it's hard to give up a dream, he had a dream of riches, power, Wall Street, he had dreamed of it all, growing up in Amory he had probably checked out books from this library as a boy, right here at the Amory Public Library, books about making money, or at least about getting into college, it was all a continuum of dreamed outcomes, the Ivy League, Wall Street, Greenwich, swimming pools, the works, it was hard to have to give up a dream, I knew that from my own life, I had dreamed of being a writer, of course I had dreams of my own, it was almost impossible to give them up, if not for Jeremy and Daphne having an affair, if not for that I might have kept struggling along, Jeremy was the real writer, he was the one who could spin stories, most of what we wrote together was his work, but ironically the one great success he had was *Catbirds*, it was my story, I had only thought it might be a good short story, but he said we should sell it, we should turn it into a screenplay, and when we broke up, when our partnership broke up, it was complicated, but we worked it out in the end, he and I ended our relationship, I moved out of the house that Daphne and I had bought years before, and when he sold *Catbirds*, I got half a story credit, it wasn't nothing, he ended up making more than I did, but for me the check was substantial, and it seemed like my marriage was done for and my career was done for, my dreams were dashed, it was something that Adam and I had in common, we each had our dreams collapse, or they were destroyed, I don't know the right term, he lost everything, I lost everything, somehow he ended up face down in an oily canal off the Housatonic River, I had survived, I had a new life, well, it was partially new, Daphne and I never divorced, we rode it out, we went to a therapist, it was a reason I had gone back to school, I was shocked that we could repair our relationship, the dog was sick, she wanted my help with him, there was something wrong with his paws and he needed to go to the vet every few weeks, she couldn't get him up into the car by herself, so I helped, I helped with the dog, Gnarls Barkley had been my dog too, when I moved out those first weeks I missed him as much as I missed Daphne, honestly, although he was always Daphne's dog, a dog is always one person's dog, I think, I always thought that, and Gnarls was Daphne's dog, he was a lab mix, a big brown lump, she fed him too much, probably that was why he paid close attention to her, he always sat near her, under the dining room table, out on the patio, even in bed, he slept on the floor on her side of the bed, of course when I moved out I couldn't take him with me, of course he would stay with her, I wasn't allowed to have a dog in the apartment building when I moved out of my home, it was a terrible place up in Sawtelle, a run-down apartment building, I never knew anyone in the building, I never looked up at anyone in the halls, I was ashamed to be there, this was another thing that Adam and I had in common, he had the Treadway apartment, I had my dreary studio in Sawtelle, it wasn't even big enough to have Muriel stay with me, but I was too ashamed to have her there at all, there was even a tire shop across the street from my Sawtelle apartment, just the way Adam had one across the street from the Treadway, if I had understood that about Adam, if I had understood that he was broke and living in the Treadway, I might have said, hey, me too, me too, Adam, I had a place like this, I lived in a crappy studio in Sawtelle, it was depressing, but I got a better place, maybe you can get a better place too, I would have told him to hang in there, well, I could imagine that, although I know he would never have listened to me, but I could imagine telling him to hang on, he would find a better place to live, I had, I had moved to a better place with an extra room for Muriel, and then Daphne and I began to see each other again, we had an odd kind of relationship for a long time, we had dinner together, we saw movies together, but we lived in separate places, she used to joke to friends, when we ran into friends, that she got all the benefits of a marriage and none of the drawbacks, no socks on the floor, she said, not that I left socks on the floor, she was joking, she would say, the perfect marriage really requires a husband and wife to live in separate abodes, we lived that way for a couple years, we went to parties together, we took care of Gnarls Barkley, we went to school fundraisers, it was strange but it worked, again, that was Daphne's line, that was what she said, it was strange but it worked, and I could have said to Adam, look, look at me, look at me, I climbed back up from a dark place, I made myself a new career, I saved my marriage, it was an unusual relationship with Daphne but it was a marriage, but of course I never said anything like that to Adam, and then it was too late to say anything, I made that one call at the beginning of the pandemic and then I went back to my own life, which was healing, healing, that's the word, it was healing, even amid the pandemic, that was the difference between Adam and me, well, there were a lot of differences but a key difference was that his life fell apart and he didn't have anyone to help him put it together, I had Daphne, I had Muriel, that was the difference I guess

Well, I had the four boxes of Adam's stuff in my car, and I had imagined letting Julia take something from them, a keepsake, I had imagined letting her look through the boxes and picking a keepsake, but the gun was in one of the boxes, it was wrapped up in a rag, and she had been traumatized by that gun, I didn't want her to see it, she would freak out, so I asked if there was anything specific she wanted to remember him by, I didn't have much, just some books and photos, but she said no, she said, I thought I would want something but now I don't think I do, and I was surprised, I said, are you sure, I said, nothing, because I knew she had come to the apartment after Adam died, the old lady down the hall had told me so, did you find the girl, she said, and I had found the girl, it was Julia, she had come to the apartment, she had tried to let herself in, so I assumed there would be something she would ask for, but she said no, even when I said, are you sure, nothing, she said she didn't want anything, and I asked her, I tried to ask her gently, but didn't you go to his apartment after he died, didn't you try to let yourself in, but she told me she hadn't wanted anything out of the apartment, no, she had been checking on him, she had heard they had found a dead man in Ogden, it worried her, she called his apartment and got no answer, so she went to the apartment and rattled the door, and when he didn't answer, she said, she was pretty sure it was Adam who had been found, he was the dead man that had been found in Ogden, the dead man who had drowned near Adam's apartment, and the police didn't know who it was, plus everyone was freaking out, she said, they were freaking out about the Wuhan virus, so she just called the police and gave an anonymous tip, she told them Adam's address and in the end that was how the police figured out that the body was Adam, it was because she had called in the information, she had at least done that for Adam, otherwise who knows what would have happened, and she was right, Adam might have gone unidentified for years, who knows, forever, if she hadn't called and said that it was probably him floating in the canal, no one else had missed him for almost two weeks, he would have been buried in a potter's field, alone, she said, and I thought, standing near the doorway of the Amory Public Library, well, at least this was better than that, we had waited too long, we had waited more than two years, still, we were remembering Adam today, what if we had never known, what if no one had ever known that he had died, this was better than that, and at that point Daphne arrived, she arrived at the last possible moment, I was glad of that, she had found a poem to read, we were both worried no one would want to speak, my mother had said she was not sure she wanted to speak at the service, too much water under the bridge, she said, she hadn't even wanted to come but Carl persuaded her that she should, and Evan was there, too, I hadn't seen him come in, and there was Muriel as well, we were all together now, all of us together, everyone that was left, my mother, me, Evan, Daphne, Muriel, that was the whole family, we were all together

Well, not Terry, Terry our half brother, I had invited him but it was a long way to come from Chicago, and he barely knew Adam, he had not seen Adam since he was a boy, so it was no surprise he wouldn't make the trip east, besides, I had visited him not long after Adam died, I had driven Adam's car across the country, I was planning on giving Adam's old car to Muriel, plus I had the four boxes of Adam's belongings, so I drove West with them, it was still fairly early in the pandemic, it was a strange time to travel, I had a bandana to wear around my face, that was all I had, I had used up my paper masks, they were still hard to find, anyway, I drove across the country with Adam's few belongings, four boxes in the back seat of the car, plus the gun was in there and I was always thinking about it, what would happen if I got pulled over and searched, I didn't have a permit, but for some reason I held on to it, I stayed at motels and at night I would bring that one box in with me, so it wasn't unattended in the car, I would check in, open the windows of the motel room, and wait outside for the room to air out, just in case, I knew that some people were wiping down doorknobs and handles with alcohol, but I didn't have any wipes, no Clorox, no alcohol, nothing like that, you couldn't find anything like that in stores at that point, so I just aired the rooms out, and I then brought in my box, Adam's box, with the gun and the photo albums, and my suitcase, and in the morning I would go out to the car, pack it up, and drive off, it took me five days, I couldn't drive more than ten hours a day, I didn't have it in me, but on the second day I was close to Chicago and I called Terry, I told him I was coming through Chicago, it wasn't really true but I was close, I asked if he would like to meet somewhere, it was strange because it was still the pandemic, there were still restrictions, but Terry didn't seem to mind, he told me to come to his apartment, he figured I was safe, that was how he put it, so I found his apartment building and went up to his place, I brought up a photo album, as it happened there was a picture in there of him, someone must have taken a picture of him at our house, he was in a room with Adam and Willie, they weren't really together but they were in the same room, I showed it to him and he looked at it for a while, he said, I think that was when I was seven years old, and I said, so Adam was five, and Willie was four, and I would have been three, although I wasn't in the picture, yes, he said, you were three the summer that I lived with your family, and I was surprised to hear this, I hadn't known Terry had ever stayed with us, especially for an entire summer, well, he said, it wasn't the whole summer, there were problems, there was a day, he said, he and Adam were doing something, they were playing in the woods, Terry told me, and Terry decided to hide, he hid beyond a rock in the woods, a boulder, and Adam looked for him, he looked for him everywhere, he was calling Terry's name, but Terry stayed quiet, crouching in the shadow of a boulder, and finally it seemed like Adam had stopped looking, Terry assumed Adam had given up, so he stood up, Terry stood up, and it turned out Adam had been there all along, he was right there by the boulder, waiting to surprise Terry, he was playing a trick, Terry said, I thought I had been playing a trick on him, but then he played a trick on me, he jumped up and frightened me, and as I listened to Terry recalling this story, I nodded, I could imagine his surprise, I felt sympathy for him, I could imagine that it would be frightening to be surprised by Adam, and then, Terry recalled, I hit him, I had a tree branch, we had been pretending to ride horses on tree branches, I swung it over my head and hit Adam right in the face, it knocked him over, and your parents sent me home again, because I had hit Adam in the face with a tree branch, just because you hit him with a branch that one time, I said, I was shocked, no, Terry said, no, it was more than that, because the next day or maybe two days later, Adam hit me with a wooden block, and then I don't remember it exactly but we got in a fight and he hit me with a jump rope, so I went back to my grandmother's, I didn't stay with your family after that, it was my fault, I'm neurodivergent, we didn't know about it at the time, I don't know why I hit him with a tree branch, I just did it, and after that we were fighting every day, we were trying to kill each other, that was what someone said, maybe it was your mother, we were trying to kill each other, so I left, my grandmother came to pick me up, I don't think I stayed with you anymore after that, but I like having this picture of me and Adam and Willie, it's nice, it makes me a little sad to look at it but it's nice

After visiting Terry, I didn't make any more stops, I just drove, ten or so hours a day, I would rest in the middle of the day, find a way to get some food, it wasn't always easy, a lot of restaurants were closed, I would look for premade sandwiches or pizza, by the fifth day I just drove without stopping, it got late but I just kept driving, I didn't want to spend another night in a motel, I wanted to get home, and I did, Daphne was there, I didn't want to wake her but she came out of the bedroom when I let myself in, I was carrying the box, the box with the gun in it, I didn't want to leave it unattended in the driveway, and she asked what I had, I said, Adam's last earthly belongings, a few photos, a few datebooks, and a handgun, and because I had told her about my conversations with my mother and with Julia, Daphne knew what the gun was, and I said, I don't know what to do with the gun, it's crazy, I've driven it clear across the country, I want to throw it away but I just don't seem to be able to do it, I'm not afraid of it anymore, it's fine now that Carl removed the bullets, it's strange to hold the gun in your hands, I said to Daphne, strange to think that Adam had held it too, that we had both held this gun in our hands, it was a German make, not that it mattered, it didn't matter about the make or the model, it was just that it came from Adam's belongings, that was what interested me, and Daphne said, she whispered, it's okay, it was late, she was half-asleep,

but she understood, she took the box from me and she made
room for it on a shelf in the closet in our bedroom, it will be
safe up there for the night, she said, then we'll figure out what
to do with it, we'll keep it here for the time being, we'll figure
out what to do with it later

And Daphne said, come and see Gnarls, he's still alive, it's like he was holding on to see you one last time, poor Gnarls, the poor old dog had lain down in the utility room, he liked to lie by the hot-water heater in there for some reason, you would think it would be warm there but what he liked was the cool concrete floor, there wasn't much room but he managed to squeeze in and lie down, there he is, Daphne said, it's the only place he feels safe now, and there wasn't room but Daphne curled up beside him on the floor in the utility closet, and she made room for me in there too, somehow there was room for both of us and the dog, I lay down beside them and I thought how grateful I was to have made it home in time to be there with Gnarls, to be there for Daphne, and it reminded me that I had not been there for Adam, I had not seen him before he died, I hadn't lain down with him the way I was doing with Gnarls and Daphne, no one had been with Adam, at least as far as I or the police knew, he had been alone in the moments before he died, but I had made it home in time for Daphne and for Gnarly, and the sound of me arriving home must have woken up Muriel, she came to the doorway of the utility room and lay down there as well, reaching in to put her hand on Gnarly's paw, and I lay there in the tiny utility closet under the blinking light of a smoke detector, the red light winking on and off at me and my family, there was room for us, that was all the room there was

Hello, thank you for coming, my name is Randy Green, I'm Adam's younger brother, for those of you who might not know me, or recognize me, thank you for coming, I've met friends of Adam's from high school, I've seen neighbors from my days growing up in Amory, I really appreciate that you have come out to remember Adam, this is the best place to remember Adam, here in Amory, this was his true home, he would want to be remembered here, and I'm remembering so much about him, being back in my hometown, I remember him running down the stairs in the morning, clomping down the stairs, no one made more noise than Adam when it came to going down the stairs in the morning, yes, people are smiling to hear me recall this about Adam, all right, I've found the thread, and Julia Slotkin isn't here, it's up to me to tell Adam's story, *he used to shout* stampede, *that was something he yelled as he ran down the stairs,* yes, they are laughing and smiling, all right, I can finish from here, I can finish Adam's story from here

Acknowledgments

Many thanks to the family members, friends, and colleagues who were the first readers of *Catbirds*:

To Raphe Elkind and Lissy Newman, who read it out loud; to Jon Fried and Deena Shoshkes, always effervescent; to Deb Koenig, who helped me see what was there; to Jeremy Epstein, who didn't like it much (an honest reader is a writer's most prized possession); to Stacy Prince, for sharp insight; to Michael Ruby, my old friend and longtime newsroom neighbor; to Cary Bickley, for intel about the movie business; and, finally, to Jane, Phin, and Zach, the big believers.

For the audiobook, thanks to Tim Loughran for advice and feedback and to Zach for help with hardware and software.

Catbirds was edited by John Rambow and final edited by Caroline Trefler. The book was designed by Kevin Barrett Kane. Thank you, all.

And thanks of course to you, reader. I wish I could thank you personally. If so moved, I hope you will recommend *Catbirds* to friends, or write a review of it online—that's how an indie book like this finds an audience, one copy at a time.

About the Author

Ezra Palmer grew up in Brooklyn and now lives in Los Angeles with his family. Originally a newspaper writer and editor, he went on to launch and run internet properties for *The Wall Street Journal* and other companies. *Catbirds* is his first novel.